DOMINANT DESIRES

THE DESIRES TRILOGY BOOK ONE

MOLLY DOYLE

CONTENTS

For my Wattpad readers,

This novel is dedicated to you. I cannot thank you enough for your support, encouragement, and love over the years. Thank you for always believing in me.

CHAPTER 1

*T*he music blares through the surround sound speakers from the front of the strip club. Blue, green, and purple neon lights illuminate the dancers on the raised platforms.

There are naked women in stilettos, dollar bills folded lengthwise through G-strings, and an uncalculatable amount of men residing in booths and chairs surrounding the stages.

There's a faint scent of warm bodies, cheap cologne, and a beer-stained floor beneath our feet. Making our way toward the back of the building, our deal has already been set in stone. A decent amount of money to last me through the next few weeks has been exchanged for sexual relations.

When we reach the private room, I raise the dim, blue light, creating a seductive ambiance. Shutting the door behind us, the man I've met only moments ago approaches me.

Groping my body, he breathes heavily against my neck. I cringe from the stench of hard liquor and tobacco on his breath, somehow managing to fight the urge of shoving him onto his ass.

Somehow.

Truth be told, this has been my occupation for far too long for me to make any rookie mistakes. This is just like any other night at the club where I have no choice but to disregard it.

"Okay," I snarl, pressing my hands against his chest to establish some distance between us.

Personal space, if he's ever heard of such a thing. Although, I don't exactly seem to get much of it with my line of work.

"Where's the cash?"

He stumbles backward with a scowl. "What?"

Swaying my hips to the side, I force a grin, playing nice. "The money."

"What money?"

"Don't play games," I say, gritting my teeth, watching as he makes himself comfortable on the black, leather sofa. "I'll need to see the cash first."

Unbuckling his belt, he chuckles. "You'll get what you're worth after, sweetheart."

"Excuse me?"

"Did I stutter?" he asks, slurring his words. "Just get that sexy ass of yours over here before I change my mind."

"Oh, fuck off."

Turning on my heel, I bolt out of the room, completely disregarding his shouting from over my shoulder.

Unbelievable.

Entering the changing room after my shift, I'm relieved to find Natalie already getting dressed. After living and working together for the past several years, she's become more like a sister to me than a best friend.

With her short, blond hair and green eyes, she's unique in every way. I'm much more average looking with my long, brown hair and light, brown eyes.

"That's awful, Sasha," she says, in remarks to what had happened to me earlier. "This is the worst timing."

"It's always when rent is due."

"So, you didn't make the rest?"

I frown, discouraged. "Close, but not close enough. That drunk bastard just had to ruin it."

"What a prick!"

"Who's a prick?" Gabby chimes in, striding into the room. She studies her reflection in the mirror, groaning. "Tonight's a fucking disaster. I can't find my hair wax anywhere."

"Heads up," I warn.

Tossing her mine, she smiles with gratitude. "Always there when I need you, Sasha."

"This guy tried pulling his cock out earlier during a private dance," Natalie explains. "It's safe to say that Sasha is traumatized."

"Oh, God," Gabby dramatically gasps. "You poor thing."

"He was definitely overserved," I say. "And repulsive."

"SOS!" Kelsey exclaims from the hall, entering the dressing room with a limp. "My heel just broke."

"Yikes," Gabby says, gesturing to her bag with a nod. "Lucky for you, I always have an extra pair."

Kelsey winks. "Teamwork makes the dream work, babe."

"All right," Natalie laughs. "We're out of here."

"Oh, don't brag," Kelsey mumbles, slipping into another pair of stilettos. "Hey, I'm craving an Italian sub from Nick's. Can you guys grab me one?"

In the midst of reapplying her lipstick, Gabby shoots her a glare. "Absolutely not," she objects. "This room is not smelling like B.O. tonight. I can't handle that God-awful smell again."

"Quit your bitching."

They continue to argue while Natalie and I turn the corner, making our way down the secluded hallway.

"I don't know, Sash," she sighs. "Sometimes, I worry."

"About what?"

"If management ever found out about us prostituting on the side, all hell would break loose."

"That's not going to happen," I say, reassuringly. "You know I won't let that happen."

"Yeah, if you say so. Let's just hope that guy keeps his drunken mouth shut."

"Any luck for you tonight?"

"No," she miserably replies. "But my regular is waiting for me."

Stepping out into the night, we're greeted by the fumes of New York City. There's exhaust from buses and trucks, the aroma of fried food in the near distance, and nearby cigarette smoke.

"And guess what?" Natalie smiles, linking her arm through mine. "He says he's going to take me to a hotel this time."

"Classy."

"Right? It's about time he spoils me," she says, playfully nudging me with her elbow. "Well, he's here. Are you going straight home?"

"Of course. Netflix is calling my name."

She rolls her eyes. "I'll see you later, babe. Don't wait up for me."

"You know I will. Stay safe, Nat."

"As always!"

THE BENCH IS cold against my thighs while I patiently wait for the bus to arrive. Eagerly checking the time on my phone, I release an aggravated breath. It's more than ten minutes late. Lovely. There's nothing worse than having to rely on public transportation, but living right in the heart of the city, this is my day and night routine.

Total nightmare.

Several minutes pass before I decide I just can't take it anymore. My heels click against the pavement with each step as I make my way to the side of the road. Sticking out my arm to hail a cab, something immediately catches my attention.

A sharp, midnight black Ferrari.

Pulling up to the curb, it comes to a stop several feet away. Without thinking about the consequence of my actions, I stride over to the elegant car, eager for a better view.

The windows are heavily tinted, barely allowing any view of the driver. Curiosity gets the best of me. Squinting my eyes, I lean down, trying to get a better look inside. When suddenly, the window rolls down, and I am frozen in place.

Thick, dark lashes surround his frozen irises. His eyes are staggering, like the stars, drawing me in to explore their endless depth. They're captivating, yet as cold as ice, pooling so deeply into my soul that they send electrical chills down my spine.

Something about this man is urging me to back away, to leave, or to run. It's warning me to not speak a single word, although it's so tempting due to how brutally handsome he is.

Not one word has been spoken and I already know I'm in deeper than I could ever imagine.

My gaze drifts down to his full, pink lips, and to his strong, pronounced jawline. Such masculine features.

He tilts his head to the side, observing my every move.

Smooth, Sasha.

Just in time, he lowers his head. Devoting his attention to the screen of his cellphone, I happen to catch a glimpse of a Rolex clasped around his wrist. Along with his expensive ride, he's also wearing a suit and tie. It's evident he's wealthy.

Maybe, he's friendly. Although, a strong intuition warns me that he's the opposite.

"Is this your car?" I ask.

"It is."

That voice.

So seductive, and throaty. My breathing hitches. I can't help but allow my gaze to take note of his muscular arms and firm chest beneath his suit. My imagination wanders.

"It's beautiful," I murmur, losing my composure.

"Appreciate it."

"Where are you headed?"

Suddenly, he lifts his head, and our eyes lock.

Oh, wow.

My insides immediately turn to mush. Those piercing, blue orbs are so intense, so sharp, they could cut you like a knife. Mesmerizing, although terrifying, in the most beautiful way.

"The Pierre."

My eyes widen. "Wow, a five-star hotel," I say, impressed, yet envious. "The most prestigious hotel in New York—"

"Listen," he arrogantly interrupts. "I'm in quite a rush—"

"Well, *Sir*," I cut him off mid-sentence, turned off by the rudeness of his tone. "I'll take the hint. Have a nice night."

Turning away, I head for the sidewalk with my dignity.

Smug bastard.

Beautiful, smug bastard.

"Wait," he calls out.

My heart leaps into my throat. For a moment, a part of me believes I must be imagining this. Without giving it any thought, I turn and look in his direction.

"Have I offended you?"

I frown, fixing the strap of my purse around my shoulder. "Well, you're a bit rude."

"Come here."

Stunned, to say the least, I wonder if I have heard him correctly.

"Sorry?" I ask.

"Come here."

Well, then. Striding back to him and his luxurious car, I can't help slipping into a daze at the passenger window.

"Do you need a ride?"

"The bus should be here soon," I say, rejecting him.

"Not necessary. Allow me to drive you home." He gestures to the door with his hand. "Get in."

"Get in?"

"Yes. I don't bite," he purrs, a gleam in his eyes. "That is, unless you want me to."

A beautiful, smug, *devious* bastard.

Hesitating to think for a moment, I ponder how I should react. This night has already been hell, and I truly don't think it could get any worse. Not for anything, but sleeping with this man would certainly be the highlight of these last few months.

Years, even.

Without questioning anything further, I find myself doing as I am told. With the dark, red leather seats and this sophisticated man sitting beside me, everything feels like a fantasy.

He offers his hand. "Jaxon."

And I can't help but stare. It's unbelievable how long his fingers are and how wide his palm is.

"Sasha Pierce." I shake my head, hating how my last name has somehow slipped.

Accepting his hand, there's a strong *zap*.

Damn static.

Releasing me from his firm grasp, he takes in the sight of my patent leather, knee-high boots.

"Are you a stripper?" he asks.

Appalled by his boldness, I silently blink at him.

"Hooker?"

"Please tell me how that's any of your fucking business," I press, a wave of embarrassment flooding over me.

"You approached me, Ms. Pierce. It wasn't the other way around."

Right.

His brows furrow. "Can you simply answer the question?"

"You're very demanding."

"You truly don't have the slightest idea."

He's such a handsome man; yet so demanding and on edge. His personality is far from welcoming and he surely doesn't make a good first impression. As cliché as it sounds, there's just something about him. There's something that draws me to him like a magnet.

His face hardens instantaneously, almost as if he has somehow read my thoughts.

"So, what if I am?"

"Well, then I have an offer."

I purse my lips, smirking. "Name your price," I say.

"Thirty thousand dollars."

CHAPTER 2

a sudden chill sweeps through me, as if a cold wind has somehow cut through the closed windows. Time seems to stop and doubt settles in, knowing there is no way he could possibly be serious.

Thirty thousand dollars.

Suddenly, I find myself fantasizing about what I could do with that kind of money. I could leave the country, and fly to a paradise island, sipping a coconut rum drink on the beach. I could pay off some of my debt, presenting myself the perfect opportunity to get back on my feet. I could invest in something, buy myself a used yet reliable vehicle, and I could catch up on my rent. There's so much I could do; it's simply endless.

My heart is pulsating and my blood turns to jet fuel. My body activates a heightened state of mental and physical awareness, yet I feel disconnected from everything but the ever-present sound of my drumming heart.

"I've been invited to attend my sister's wedding in California. I've announced that I've gotten engaged a few months back, to get my loving yet overbearing parents off my back, and in doing so I've put myself into a bit of a situation.

My supposed fiancée is now invited to attend as my date, and of course I'd rather have someone play along than to admit my deceit."

Everything around me begins to spin.

"Is this a joke?" I ask, doubtful. "You seriously have thirty grand just lying around to give away?"

"Edwards. Jaxon Edwards," he says, briefly hesitating to see if it rings any bells. I remain quiet, staring at him, dumbfounded. "I'm the CEO of Edwards Enterprises, along with several other corporations worldwide."

"Several?"

He nods.

I laugh. "What are you, a millionaire?"

"Billionaire, precisely."

My jaw drops.

"I need someone to pose as my fiancée for the six months I'll be in California. We'll make appearances as needed, attend the wedding, and after the six months is up, you'll return home with thirty thousand. I believe that's a fair deal in exchange for your time."

"California is pretty far."

"It's where my family lives. I own a house there on the beach."

"For six months?" I ask.

He crookedly grins. "Are you interested?"

"Yes," I rush out.

Yes, yes, yes.

"Let's make this more interesting, then. Shall we?"

My heart hammers.

"Tell me what you know about the BDSM community," he says, his voice low.

Stirring in my seat, I fidget with my hands on my lap. BDSM? Well, I know I've watched a few intense pornos on the matter. It reminds me of the time I once was asked to belittle a man during sex. He was turned on by being degraded, and even asked me to tell him that his parents never loved him.

Shaking the memory away, my cheeks become flushed.

"Bondage, kinky sex. Sadism. Does that sound about right?"

"Any personal experience?" he asks.

"No," I begin, barely any sound to my voice. "I don't have experience, but what exactly does this have to do with anything?"

Jaxon remains silent, watching me vigilantly.

And finally, it clicks.

"I'd like for you to submit to me during your stay."

"Submit," I echo, while his eyes feverishly explore mine. "You want me to be your sex slave?"

"Submissive," Jaxon Edwards corrects. "This is consensual, Sasha, between both parties. If you will accompany me back to my hotel suite, then we can discuss this further."

"You're asking me to go up to your hotel room after telling me you're into Sadism?"

"I'm not holding you captive, Ms. Pierce. You can leave at any given moment. However, I'd love to claim you as mine."

Claim me?

I'm at a loss for words. I can hardly breathe. I'm so upset that this is happening, and I'm even more upset that it's bothering me so much. Why should I care? I allow men to use my body as a prostitute. Although, there's one huge difference here.

What I have with my clients is considered regular sex. *Vanilla*, far from kinky. I'm the one in charge of what I will and will not do. I tell men how it's going to be, and when it's going to end.

This man sitting beside me is a Dominant. I would be giving up everything I've ever known to learn something entirely different. Truthfully, I don't know if I'd be able to handle that.

Mr. Edwards pulls back onto the road without warning.

"Is this what you do?" I sarcastically question. "Pick up random women on the side of the road and ask them to become your Submissive?"

A smirk plays at his lips. "There's a first for everything."

"Oh, is there?"

"I don't prefer to waste time." He flashes me an intense glance for a moment, before turning away. "If I want something, I go for it, and in most cases, I get it. It's as simple as that."

His car comes screeching to an abrupt stop as we arrive at a set of lights. As I turn to look at him, he's already staring.

"I can't say yes until I learn more," I firmly say.

"I'll explain whatever you'd like to know once we're situated in my hotel suite. I'd rather not have this discussion in the car."

"Fine."

"I'm a man with certain needs, Sasha, and I hope you can fulfill them. If not, this arrangement can't and will not happen. Understand?"

"This is more than just me posing as your fiancée. You want me to be a lady and your fake future wife-to-be around your family, and then when it's just you and I, you want me to be your slave."

"Fuck," he growls. "I don't refer to my Subs as slaves."

"Well, at least we're on the same page, because I'm not agreeing to be anyone's slave."

We say nothing further for the rest of the drive to The Pierre. He parks his car under the large, outdoor roof beside the parking Valet.

"Wait here."

Jaxon Edwards makes his way to my door, and opens it for me like the perfect gentleman.

"Thank you," I breathe, flustered.

"Of course, Ms. Pierce."

Placing my hand on his, his grip is firm. Tight. Struggling to catch my breath, I exit his Ferrari, and he closes the door behind me. I begin to walk toward the sidewalk in a daze, until he jerks me backward, bringing me against his chest.

Our eyes lock.

"Watch your step," he warns.

Glancing down, I notice the curb I've almost tripped over. "Right," I mutter. "Thanks."

He smirks.

"Mr. Edwards," The Valet says, beaming. "How are you this fine evening, Sir?"

"Great, thank you. My bags are in the backseat. I'd like them taken up to my suite."

"Yes, Mr. Edwards." He bows in his direction, and I snort under my breath. "Of course."

Jaxon Edwards pulls out his thick wallet and doesn't bother hiding the hundred-dollar bills resting inside. The employee becomes ecstatic as he accepts his tip.

Billionaires.

"Thank you. It's much appreciated," Mr. Edwards says.

He bows once more.

"What are you, royalty?"

He ignores me and steps closer, wrapping his arm around my waist. His cologne is strong, heady. Intoxicating.

Once we reach the front desk in the lobby, they continue to treat this man like he's a King, while I feel like a nobody. It's drastic how different our lives truly are.

Making our way toward the elevators, I take in our surroundings, stunned with how beautiful this hotel is. The floors are marble, the walls are painted into complex patterns, and the ceiling is higher than imaginable.

The doors open with a *ding*. He tightens his grasp around my waist and we enter the elevator, and a couple almost joins us.

Almost.

"Pardon me," Jaxon announces, the man's eyes widening with recognition. "Would you both mind waiting for the next elevator? My date is feeling quite sick. Not knowing if it's contagious, I think it would be best if you caught the next one."

"Yes, of course. I apologize greatly for intruding," he pauses, intimidated, almost. "Jaxon Edwards?"

"Yes."

"It's a pleasure to meet your acquaintance," he says, holding out his hand, and Jaxon accepts. "I am a big admirer. Your generous donation to the Lateheart Organization was truly remarkable."

Jaxon politely grins. "I believe it was the right thing to do for such an important charity."

"Oh, it was. Outstanding. I hope you have a great night, Mr. Edwards."

He smiles. "Appreciate it. You, as well."

The elevator doors shut, and I immediately pull away.

"Wow, I've underestimated you. I can't believe all these people, bowing to you, practically worshipping the ground you walk on. It's ridiculous, really—"

Before I know it, he has me pinned up against the wall of the elevator, his hand pressed lightly against my throat.

"That god damn mouth of yours," he breathes. "Tempting me to fuck it senseless, are you?"

Jaxon Edwards pushes his waist against mine, and he trails his hands over my hips. Suddenly, he pulls up my dress and reveals my exposed lower half. A moan escapes me as he steps closer.

His palms are on fire against my cold, pale skin. "You have such a great ass."

He takes my wrists in one hand, and holds them against the mirror above my head.

I gasp. "What are you doing?"

"Quiet," he commands.

His large erection grows against my thigh, and my nipples strain in my bra. My core pulses with need, an undeniable longing, and my senses become heightened to a whole new level.

It feels so nice to be this close to someone that smells so enticing, unlike the usual, cheap beer and fake cologne.

Mr. Edwards leans down, his lips beside my ear.

"Your skin feels like velvet," he says, his voice low, tight. I shudder against him. "I want to press my lips against every inch of your body."

An involuntary moan escapes me. "Mr. Edwards—"

"Fuck," he groans, warmth sizzling down my spine. "The temptation to fuck you right in this elevator is nearly overpowering me."

Suddenly, I'm pushing myself against him, desperate to feel him. To feel *more*.

He releases my wrists, and I tightly grip his jacket, pulling him closer. Staring down at me, he examines the lust plastered across my face. There's heat in those intimidating, blue orbs, locking me in place, sending me into an infinite trance.

"Oh, Sasha," he quietly says, stroking my hair. "The things I'd do to you."

Jaxon pulls down my dress without warning. He steps back, smoothing out his suit and adjusting his tie to perfection.

And he smirks. "Unfortunate."

"Care to elaborate?" I breathlessly ask.

"I only fuck my Subs. I advise you to think very thoroughly about this arrangement. Here's a chance to leave before we step inside my suite. Otherwise, I'll be waiting for you down the hall."

The doors open with a *ding*, and he gracefully exits the elevator. I'm left standing alone, with nothing other than my wet thighs, puckered nipples, and taunting thoughts.

CHAPTER 3

*E*xiting the elevator, I turn right, spotting Mr. Edwards leaning against a wall near the door to his suite. My heels click loudly against the floor tile, and there's an echo with each step. My heart is thumping wildly against my ribcage and my ears begin ringing, a low pitch buzzing sound I can't seem to get rid of.

Staring Mr. Edwards straight in his eyes, I attempt to prove to him that he doesn't scare or intimidate me.

When in all reality, he does.

He straightens his posture. "Welcome back, Ms. Pierce."

"Are we going to stand out here all night?"

His eyes flash amusement. "Demanding little thing, aren't you?"

Reaching into his pants he retrieves the key card, sliding it fast in one swift motion. Once the door unlocks, he fixes his eyes on mine, watching me feverishly.

"After you."

"Thanks," I humor him, entering the suite.

The walls are painted a soft peach color, which is very easy on the eyes. After kicking off my heels, the carpet, a dark beige, is soft on my feet. There's a marble coffee table resting in the middle of the room, along with two couches, and a large television mounted on the wall.

He presses his hand against the small of my back, and a shiver travels down my spine. Without my heels Jaxon Edwards now towers over my five-foot-four frame, easily past six feet.

He takes notice of my bare feet. "I'm glad to see that you've made yourself at home."

The heat from his hand radiates against my skin, and my body tenses from his touch. I can't even put into words how incredible it feels to be touched by someone so powerful.

I look away from his gaze.

There's a beautiful chandelier hanging from the ceiling in the dining area. The table is long, silverware all set out along with six chairs.

Suddenly, a knock sounds from the other room.

"Excuse me, Sasha. That should be my bags with my belongings. Make yourself comfortable," he says, dismissing himself from the room.

Stepping into the guest room, I sigh comfortably at the size of the bed, as it's much bigger than mine. Standing before the large window, I am in awe, taking in the fascinating view of New York City.

A flashback of my parents comes rushing back to me, thinking back to when I was thirteen and we had all gone on a vacation.

We stayed at a hotel and had the most incredible view of a sunset, and we couldn't believe how vivacious the sight before us was. That was the last time I stood in front of a window this big. We couldn't believe how lucky we were to be seeing something so magnificent together.

Now, I'm standing alone.

The master bedroom has me in pure disbelief as I step inside. The king-sized bed has me fantasizing. Naughty,

naughty thoughts. I find myself picturing Jaxon Edwards naked, and my face blushes at the images in my head.

Sheepishly turning around, I nearly knock myself over as I bump into something. Large, firm hands grasp my arms to keep me steady.

"Are you all right?" Mr. Edwards asks.

"Yeah. I'm fine."

"A bottle of wine should arrive shortly."

"Okay," I say, following behind him.

After sitting quietly in the living room for the last several minutes, the loud knocking on the door startles me. Jaxon gracefully stands and makes his way across the room.

Opening the door, a man with a cart stands before him with a bottle of wine and a bucket of ice. After Jaxon rolls the cart further into the room, he retrieves two glasses from the dining area.

Swiftly opening the bottle, he fills our glasses halfway.

"Drink," Jaxon orders, handing me the glass as I take a small sip. "Tell me what you think."

"The best wine I've ever had," I admit.

"Excellent." He places his glass onto the table in front of us. "Excuse me for a moment. I'm going to take a few of my bags to my room, and I'll bring you the contract."

My stomach drops. "Contract?"

"Yes. Contract."

He retrieves two suitcases before leaving the room.

With sudden fear of the unknown, I rush to my feet and feel myself becoming sick. I pace around the living room only to find there's a balcony, fresh air sounding perfect.

My stomach finally starts to settle as I take a deep breath of the warm air, easing my nerves. What a sight is right before my very eyes. The tall buildings are lit up, and the sounds of the city below us are roaring; cars, sirens, and the wind.

"Beautiful out here, isn't it?" His voice startles me as I turn to face him, and he's leaning in the open doorway. I remain silent. "What's the matter?"

"Nothing," I reply.

Turning my back to him, I place my arms on the balcony rails and take another sip of my wine that must have cost him a fortune. I feel his breath against the back of my neck, and goosebumps rise on my skin. I breathe in, realizing how close he must be.

"Talk to me."

"I'm fine."

"No," he says, adamant. "Tell me what you're thinking. I don't prefer to make repeating myself a habit."

"Just give me the contract."

His eyes narrow, and he steps closer. "Why won't you tell me what's on your mind?"

"I need to talk to someone about this first, like my friend Natalie—"

He shakes his head, dismissively. "You can't tell anyone about this arrangement. This is highly confidential."

A soft whimper leaves me, vulnerability hitting me hard. As he turns around I inhale a long and anxious breath, before I silently follow Mr. Edwards back into his suite.

Resting on the living room table are the papers, the papers that will define whether not I chose to stay or leave. Instead of sitting, he remains standing, holding his glass of wine, keeping his gaze intently on my every move. I sit on the couch and cross my legs, placing my glass onto the table.

"Can I ask you a few questions first?"

He sits beside me and makes himself comfortable. "Of course. Anything. But please, expect complete honesty. You may or may not like what you hear."

"You're a Dominant. What does that mean?"

He takes a quick sip of his wine. "It means I want you to willingly surrender yourself to me. Mind, body, and soul."

"Surrender?" I chew on my bottom lip. "What is a Submissive?"

"A Submissive is a person who makes a conscious choice to give up some, or all, control of her life to another person. To allow someone else to control your body and behavior within the preset limits in which are agreed upon by both parties."

"That sounds a lot like a slave."

"No. Submission is not only about rough, kinky sex, and chains and whips, although those things can and do play a part. It is much deeper than that. It comes from the heart. I know that might be difficult for you to understand, but submission is a choice. It will be a wonderful gift to me as your Dominant."

"Noted."

"You will do whatever I require of you, of course within the boundaries we've agreed upon. You'll serve me in whatever manner I wish, for my pleasure and my own comfort. When you behave, I will reward you. If you disobey me, I will punish you. That needs to be clear. Are you still with me, Ms. Pierce?"

I nod, swallowing hard. "Yes."

"Serving can also take many other forms too, such as cleaning, cooking, taking care of my house or running errands. You'll accompany me on outings as well. I don't consider my Subs my slaves. You need to wrap your head around that."

"How many women have there been?" I question, and his jaw tightens. "Just curious."

"Twenty-three."

The moment I stand, a look of concern crosses his features.

"I don't know, Mr. Edwards. I haven't even heard anything regarding your rules yet. I'm getting light-headed from overthinking, or maybe it's just the wine."

"Christ," he breathes, joining me across the room. "I figured this would be easy for you, considering your line of work, that is."

"Sorry to disappoint," I argue, forcing a laugh. "I'm under-qualified for this, really, I am—"

"That may be true, Sasha," he says, searching my eyes with heated passion. "Although, I'm always up for a challenge."

My nerves instantly kick in. "Maybe," I reply.

"You look exhausted. Sleep on it." He holds out his hand to me, and it takes me a few agonizing seconds before I accept. "You'll sleep in the guest room."

"Oh?"

"I chose to not share a bed with my Subs."

We reach the door of the guest room.

"Is there a reason for that, Mr. Edwards?" I ask.

"There is. This is a different type of relationship," he explains, briefly hesitating. "Sleeping together leans more on an emotional connection, a different bond, and that's not what I'm searching for. Besides, I like my space."

"And I like mine," I reply.

His eyes narrow, and he nods. "Goodnight, Ms. Pierce. I look forward to seeing you in the morning."

Turning away, he appears to be distracted.

Pushing open the bathroom door, I sleepily strip off my clothes. The water trails down my body, my muscles finally relaxing from how tense I've become. I try desperately to let my mind go blank, so I don't have to think about this deal I'm being offered, but it's impossible.

Turning off the lights in the guest room, crawling sleepily into bed, I'm left pondering about the other end of this.

Thirty thousand dollars. It's worth it. I'll have the money.

But most of all, I'll have *him*.

WAKING up to a gentle breeze against my skin, there's a

blinding light shining in through an opened window. Slowly opening the door, I peek my head through the doorway.

There's a dull silence.

After making my way down the hall, I realize Mr. Edwards is nowhere to be found.

Standing only inches away from the master bedroom, I finally gather the courage to knock on the door, and there's no answer.

Since the door is slightly cracked, I open it further, and the sound of running water is heard. Without thinking it through, I find myself peaking inside the bathroom.

My gaze locks on the shower, the thin wall of glass allowing a blurry outlining of his body. His ass appears firm, and I can almost see the tone of muscle in his arms and back, while his hand runs through his hair. He is perfection.

God-like.

"Good morning, Ms. Pierce." His voice unexpectedly echoes, bringing me back to reality. "Did you sleep well?"

Embarrassment strikes me hard as I tuck a strand of hair nervously behind my ear.

"Yes, very well," I stammer.

The water stops running.

"I'm happy to hear that. Would you mind handing me that towel?"

Standing close, I hand him the towel and look away just in time, before he has the chance to step into my view.

The moment I look back to him, my heart races. The water drips softly down his hair. With his broad shoulders, solid chest, and toned abdomen, my knees feel like they are moments away from buckling.

My gaze travels down further, and I lay my eyes above the towel wrapped around his waist, enhancing the curve at his hips.

And it slips. "Oh, God."

"Not quite. Just me."

I'm rushing out of the bathroom before I know it, waiting patiently on the couch as the minutes pass by.

"For God's sake, Richard." Jaxon sounds outraged as he enters the room. "This was an utter waste of my time. It was your job to inform me about this yesterday the moment you had an official statement regarding the changed date. I'm done with this."

With that, he ends the call.

"Is everything all right?"

Jaxon Edwards has on a pair of nice, black dress pants along with a collared, dark blue, button-up long sleeve shirt.

"It appears I won't be staying in New York after all. You need to decide by five o'clock. Today."

He slips his arms through his suit jacket, shrugging it on.

"Where is it, Mr. Edwards?"

"Where you left it."

Right.

My gaze meets the binding contract resting lifelessly on the table. I blink at him, unsure what to say. My hands are fidgeting on my lap, my palms are clammy, and all the color drains from my face. *Thirty thousand dollars*, I remind myself.

Who knew that such tiny, black words typed out on a piece of paper could have such a drastic impact on my life.

Jaxon Edwards sits beside me, and finally, I begin to read.

*a*s I stare down at the contract before me, I try desperately to seem untouched with what I have read. What do I say? Slowly lifting my head, our eyes meet.

Something inside me instantly changes.

I've never felt more alive. It's as if every neuron in my brain is erupting. Instead of feeling numb, I feel rejuvenated.

"Do you have any questions?"

"Okay," I blurt out.

"Okay?"

"Yes, Mr. Edwards. I'll do it."

He begins to stand. "I'll get a pen."

"Wait," I rush out, and he stills. "Not yet. I don't want to sign anything until I see where I'll be staying, and I want to know you for more than just an hour."

He appears amused with my regulations.

"After all, this is all about trust. Isn't it?"

He nods, impressed. "Trust is highly important."

"Good. So, you understand."

"I understand completely." He rests his ankle over his knee, spreading an arm over the head of the couch. "There is no rush for this. I want nothing more than for you to feel comfortable."

"There's one thing I'm not okay with."

"That's fine. We can go over the entire length of the contract whenever you're ready. We'll need to discuss hard limits, soft limits, and boundaries. It would be best to discuss what you are and are not comfortable with, especially since this is a first for you. As I've said before, this is consensual."

Placing the papers on the table, I nod. "I need to get this out of the way now, Mr. Edwards."

Reaching forward, he delicately folds up the contract, and secures it into the pocket of his suit.

When his eyes meet mine, I freeze.

"Yes?" he encourages, smiling. "You were saying?"

Those straight, pearly whites are on perfect display, the worst distraction. I anxiously blink at him, trying to collect my thoughts.

"I don't kiss."

His brows furrow, and his smile fades. "You don't kiss?"

"I don't," I firmly state, setting our first boundary. "I don't like mixing business with personal life, if that makes any sense."

Smirking, he rubs his fingers along his jaw. "Are you implying that you're not dying to kiss me, Ms. Pierce?"

My gaze wanders to his lips. Those full, plush lips. I stare at them, my stomach turning over.

Well, I'm not so sure.

"Breakfast." Mr. Edwards stands, adjusting his collar. "I'm assuming you must be hungry."

"Starving," I admit.

"Great, as am I." He grins, and I make my way to the door where he's waiting, slipping into my heels. "There's this great little café downtown I'd like to take you to."

"Which one?"

"Sasha?"

As I lift my head, his eyes burn into mine. They hold so much mystery I'm left spellbound. He's quiet, making me wait.

I can hardly bear it.

"Yes?" I softly ask.

"I don't kiss, either, for the same reason."

Shocked by his statement, I remain silent, speechless.

The truth is, I assumed nobody else would ever have the same perception as me on the matter. Before I can even reply, he holds the door open and motions with his hand for me to exit his suite.

"After you."

Mr. Edwards brings me to a very fancy café downtown, and we are treated like royalty. Once we've finished eating breakfast, we head over to my apartment, and I show him to the restroom.

The sink in the kitchen is filled with dishes. This place is an absolute disaster. Embarrassment washes over me. Frantically turning on the faucet, my hand hovers over the sponge, and I become still.

What am I doing?

I'm about to fly all the way across the country with a man I hardly know, a stranger. This is very unlike me. Everything I've ever done in my life has always been planned, well thought out. Now, I'm being reckless. I feel like I'm losing my mind.

Feeling a presence behind me, I turn off the faucet, turning around to find Jaxon watching me.

Reading me.

"Do you want anything to drink?" I quietly ask.

He shakes his head. "No."

"Are you hungry?"

"No."

"We don't have much food, but I can cook something. I just have to do the dishes first—"

"We've just eaten breakfast," he interrupts, brows furrowed. "What's wrong?"

Mr. Edwards seems to stare right through me. I lower my gaze to the floor, chewing nervously on my lip. Gently placing his finger beneath my chin, he lifts my head.

"What's the matter?"

"It's nothing."

Anger crosses his beautiful features. "What the fuck do you mean, nothing?"

"I just can't believe I'm doing this."

"Ah, yes. I bet you're very dismayed to leave this luxury apartment you've got here."

"Wow." I grimace at him, offended. "Well, not all of us are lucky enough to live in mansions and have private jets as a form of travel."

"Are you ready?"

This is it.

Everything in me warns me to not leave with him. Red flags are raised, and my body ignites in a rush of adrenaline.

Am I ready?

"Yes," I reply.

"Wonderful. Do you need help with packing your bags?"

"No, thanks. I think I'm capable of doing that myself—" Suddenly, he heads toward Natalie's room. "Stop."

"I'm assuming this isn't your room?"

With that, he walks toward mine.

Rushing around him, I stand in front of the door, blocking the entrance.

"A little privacy here, Jaxon. I'd like to pack my shit by myself. You can go downstairs or wait in the car."

Slamming his hands against the door, my head between his arms, he locks me in place.

"I do believe I've advised you to not make giving me orders a habit."

Without warning, he pins my arms above my head. His body leans into mine, and the scent of his cologne washes over me. The way he's touching me, the way he smells, this man is irresistible.

I can't get enough.

His lips press against my neck, and a muffled moan escapes me. The tip of his tongue trails over the sensitive skin beneath my earlobe, and I drown in sheer satisfaction.

"Jaxon," I moan, writhing against him. "You have to stop."

"I won't stop," he breathes against my neck. "Not until you're pleading for mercy."

The moment I attempt to gain back control of my arms, he grips them tighter. I am held hostage.

"It's taking so much self-control for me to not fuck you right against this goddamn door."

His erection grows bigger beneath his dress pants, as he places his knee between my thighs, spreading my legs. The chemistry between us is uncanny, undeniable. My nipples harden, straining against my bra. Arching my back, I press my body closer to his.

When unexpectedly, the front door opens, and Natalie's gaze meets mine.

CHAPTER 5

"*N*atalie."

Mr. Edwards releases me, and turns to face her.

Her eyes widen, and her mouth falls partially open. It's clear she's staggered by his appearance in our shit-box apartment.

"Hi there," she chirps, and he holds out his hand between them. Natalie stares at it, enthralled.

"Pleasure," Mr. Edwards says.

Placing her hand in his, she dramatically sighs, and a blush settles on her cheeks.

"The pleasure is all mine," she flirtatiously says.

He smirks. "I've heard a lot about you, Natalie."

"Have you?" she asks, momentarily glancing at me.

I turn to Jaxon, and our eyes lock. Once more, I become breathless, flustered.

"This is my roommate, well, more like sister," I explain, quickly looking away. "And this is Mr. Edwards. Jaxon. He's, well—" I hesitate, taking note of his calm and collected composure, not having the slightest idea on what to address him as.

He places his hand onto my lower back. "I'm an old friend."

My lips part, and my legs become weak.

Get yourself together.

"Oh, that's nice," Natalie responds. "From where, high school? Because I've known Sasha for a while, and I'm sure that I've never seen, or at least heard about you before. Until now, that is."

"Nat, he's a friend," I quietly mumble. "No interrogations."

"Sorry," she playfully smiles. "I don't mean to pry. It's just me and my overprotective nature, I guess."

"I can assure you, you have nothing to worry about." Mr. Edwards reassures her with a grin. "I'll take good care of her."

"Oh?" she questions. "Are you leaving?"

"Just for a little bit," I begin to say.

"Six months," he chimes in. "I've offered her a position as my personal assistant. She'll be residing with me in California for the time being."

"Wait," I rush out. "I don't even think this is plausible. I have to help with my share of the rent—"

"Not a problem," he speaks over me. "I'll write out a check, Ms. Pierce."

This is insane. This man is insane. . .

About *me*.

"It was great meeting you, Natalie. Sasha speaks highly of you. Although, we should really get going. The jet will be arriving soon. I'll help you gather your belongings, Sasha."

"No, it's all right. She'll help me pack."

Mr. Edwards turns his head, those piercing blue eyes locking with mine. There's an eerie silence for a moment, and I can feel my pulse increase with each passing second.

Finally, I come to realize that he must be warning me to not speak a single word about our deal.

"Don't worry," I reassure him. "I'll meet you outside once I'm ready. It shouldn't take too long."

"I'll be by my car."

He flashes one last grin in her direction, and closes the door behind him.

"Oh my god," Natalie shrieks, while I quickly shush her. "You bitch! I am so fucking jealous!"

"Why?"

"Uh, hello?" she sarcastically sings. "Because you're fucking Mr. tall, dark, and handsome! That's why!"

"Lower your voice," I urge. "You're so damn loud."

"And I care, why?"

"He already has quite the ego. That man doesn't need to think any higher of himself."

She rolls her eyes. "It's not fair for a man to be that good looking. Is he a client? How much does he pay?"

"No, he's not a client, and he doesn't pay for sex, because I'm not sleeping with him."

She frowns, folding her arms across her chest. "And why not?"

"Surely, he doesn't need to pay anyone to sleep with him," I dryly mutter. "The man is a billionaire. Literally. I stayed with him in his suite at the Pierre last night."

"What!" she squeals, bursting into laughter. "Well, at least one of us is doing something right. You're sipping champagne at the Pierre, while I'm drinking room temperature beer at a shitty motel, faking moans all night for a fat slob."

I anxiously chew on my lip.

"Listen. I saw the two of you," she says. "You can't deny it. He had your hands above your head, had you pinned to the wall, and was practically devouring your neck. I completely ruined your moment."

"It's fine, really."

"You can't tell me there's nothing there. He wants you, Sash."

I enter my bedroom and she follows close behind. Opening the drawer of my dresser, I pull out as many pairs of panties that I own. Natalie grunts from behind me.

"Wear those silky, red ones. He will die when he sees you in those. You're drop-dead gorgeous."

"I'm only his assistant," I press. "That is all. I told him that."

She snorts. "Yeah, whatever. Like that's believable."

"Just help me pack."

Once I'm finished packing, I change into a comfortable dress. Taking in my surroundings, it finally hits me that I won't see this place again for six months. For that, I'm grateful.

"You have to keep me posted on everything," she pleads.

Facing Natalie, I smile.

"Of course," I reply, accepting her tight embrace. "I'm going to miss you. Are you sure you'll be okay?"

"Don't worry about me. I'm a big girl."

"He says he'll be writing out a check, so at least you don't have to worry about my share of the rent. I'm getting good money for being his assistant. In the meantime, if you need any help, any at all, you have to let me know."

She laughs, pushing me toward the door. "I'm fine."

"Well, I'll call you when I land."

She sadly gawks at me. "His own private jet? Shit, I would kill to be in your shoes right now. Get laid for me."

Oh, I will.

You have no idea.

Shutting the door behind me, I'm trying desperately to calm my erratic thoughts. Dragging my heavy-as-shit suitcase down the hall as quickly as I can, nearly tripping on my own feet, a quiet chuckle disrupts me.

Mr. Edwards is standing a few doors down, waiting

patiently, with his back pressed against the wall. His arms are folded over the front of his suit, and he's staring humorously in my direction.

I deeply sigh.

"Need some help?" he asks. "Allow me."

"I've got it," I respond, until he takes the handle of the suitcase right out of my grasp. "I thought I told you to wait outside."

"That fucking mouth of yours," he sharply exhales, turning away. "I don't know who you think you're talking to. I don't take orders from anyone. I give them."

"Yeah, well, I'm not your Submissive just yet."

He laughs at my remark, and we head toward the elevator.

"You have no clue how difficult it is for me to not place you over my knee, and spank your ass raw."

"What's holding you back?"

He shoots me an intense stare, eyes narrowed. "You've yet to sign my contract, Ms. Pierce."

Anticipation overwhelms me as we step into the elevator. The memory of last night at the Pierre comes to mind, our heated encounter of him pinning me against the wall. A part of me wonders if it will happen again.

Although, this time, he doesn't move an inch.

CHAPTER 6

There's a long silence between us. Jaxon pulls over to the gate of a private airport, where a man in business attire stands formally. After a few seconds, and a courteous nod, the gate opens. We come to a stop near a runway, and instantly, I am struck with awe.

Edwards Enterprises is printed across the large, black jet.

This is surreal.

He opens his door. "Stay here."

Stepping out into the warm air to get a better view, I gaze at the jet in amazement.

"Did I not make myself clear?" he growls, forcefully shutting my door.

"I can open it myself, thanks."

A man strides toward us. "Good afternoon, Mr. Edwards. How are you?"

"Peachy," he mutters, glaring at me.

"Can I be of any help with gathering her belongings, Sir?"

"No, that's okay," I reply. "But thank you for the offer—"

"That would be great, Ronald," Jaxon speaks over me.

Holding out his hand, he stares at me with intense eyes.

That dull ache returns between my legs. I've never been more aroused in my life.

Placing my hand in his, we walk up the steps, and he leads me inside. It's beautiful, and beyond elegant. I am mesmerized.

Mr. Edwards rests his hand against the small of my back, directing me toward what appears to be the living area. Taking in my new surroundings, I am in a trance, envious. When suddenly, I hear an unfamiliar voice from behind us.

"Mr. Edwards, it's nice to see you again." Her words slip out in a purr, as she slightly leans forward to enhance her perky breasts, and pretty, blue eyes. "When would you like to take off, Sir?"

"Within the next few minutes," he bleakly responds. "I'd like for you to meet my new business partner, Ms. Pierce. And Sasha, this is Sofia. She's our co-pilot." He looks forward, meeting her lustful gaze once more. "Please tell Roger I say hello."

She bats her eyelashes, blushing. "Certainly," she replies, stepping closer. "I will inform him that you'd like to depart within the next few minutes."

"Thank you, Sofia."

"Absolutely."

With that, she smiles, striding away as she sways her hips.

"Right this way," Mr. Edwards says, and I follow closely behind him.

Facing me, he gestures for me to sit in the black, leather seat beside the window. Doing as I'm instructed, I begin to make myself comfortable, and he fastens the seatbelt for me.

"Question," I carefully say. "Do you mind?"

His eyes set on mine. "Not at all."

"Have you slept with her?" I nonchalantly ask, his eyebrow raising. "Your co-pilot?"

He smirks, amused. "Am I sensing jealousy?"

"Absolutely not."

"I don't have casual, sexual relations. Especially not with personnel."

My world begins to spin, confusion overtaking me. No casual sex relations? Surely, he wasn't being dishonest or exaggerating when he said he only lives by the BDSM lifestyle.

He sits beside me, and it's not long before we take off. Gripping the armrests, my body tenses. Little does he know, this is the first time I've ever been on an airplane.

About thirty minutes later, the seat belt signs turn off, and it's smooth sailing. The tour of the airplane leaves me even more astonished. There're so many rooms to explore, including an office, a space for business meetings, a full bar, and even a dining area.

"This is ridiculous. You could live here."

He glances at me. "I could."

"Next, you're going to tell me you have a casino."

"Gambling is not exactly my forte," he replies, smirking.

We stop abruptly at another door. The moment I enter the room, I can't help becoming curious. It's a bedroom. Although, it appears to be meant for a female.

"This room," I hesitate, turning to face him. "Who is it for?"

His eyes project an imminent longing, an undeniable hunger. He allows his gaze to travel to my lips, to my cleavage, and my hips.

Although his facade is intimidating, as he's most certainly in his Dominant mindset, there's something about this moment that leaves me wanting more. Much more.

"It's meant for your submissive." I immediately look away. "This is where I would sleep if I travel on business with you, isn't it?"

He nods in response, watching me intently.

Stepping further inside, I lower myself onto the bed. My fingertips trace the soft, white comforter, and my eyes close.

Drifting into a different world, I slightly draw back the covers, fisting the satin sheets.

My eyes open, and Jaxon is only inches away.

"What are you doing?" I innocently ask, cheeks flushed.

"Nothing," he answers. "Standing by my word."

Even though I hate to admit it, I find it more than difficult to convince myself that I don't want to submit to this man. It's as if you can feel an electrical current in the room.

A spark.

A craving, an indescribable need.

He turns away.

TURBULENCE AWAKES me from my deep slumber. There's a lightweight blanket draped over me, and it appears to be night as I glimpse through the windows.

"Shit," I whisper, sitting upright.

"Sleep well?"

Jaxon sits several feet away, holding a glass of red wine.

Without saying a word, I nod.

He stands, placing his glass onto the table. "Would you like a glass?"

"Please."

The wine is astringent, leaving my mouth dry, yet the finish is more than delightful. After nearly drinking the entire glass, my head becomes lighter, and I'm stunned to already feel a slight buzz.

"How long was I asleep?" I ask.

"A few hours." The ringing of his cellphone sounds, and he reaches into the pocket of his suit. "I have to take this. Excuse me."

After pouring another glass of wine, a vinyl record player catches my attention. I haven't seen one of these in ages. Music begins to play, and I've never felt more alive. I feel strong, untouchable, and the alcohol only seems to boost my confidence levels even higher.

Swaying my hips to the rhythm, I'm careless and free as we fly through the dark sky. It can't get any better than this.

The song's pace quickens. I close my eyes, letting myself go. Spinning in circles with the glass still in my hand, I run my other hand all over my body. My imagination wanders.

I imagine Mr. Edwards caressing me, cornering me against a wall with his hand against my throat. Stripping my clothes, pushing his length into me, claiming me.

Slipping a hand into my bra, my fingers pinch my puckered nipple. A hushed moan escapes from my lips, wetness pooling between my inner thighs. I am drenched at the thought of him.

When my eyes open, my heart sinks.

Jaxon Edwards stands several feet away, and his eyes are narrowed, raging with *dominant desires*. Immediately, I become still, mortified that he has intruded.

"I didn't know you were there," I rush out, embarrassed. "How long were you watching me?"

Turning on my heel, I silence the music.

"Does that truly matter?"

As I face him, he takes a seat on the end of the couch, crossing his ankle over his knee.

"Continue," he murmurs. "Don't let me stop you."

His lips remain parted while he continues to keep his eyes locked with mine. Daring me. Testing me. All the color drains from my face and goosebumps rise on my skin. I begin to feel the wine swirling around in my stomach, threatening to come back up.

He spreads his arms out on the head of the couch. "Forget it, Ms. Pierce. Just wanted to have a little fun, is all."

"You want me to touch myself in front of you, Mr. Edwards?" I ask, putting him on the spot. He appears amused, cocking his head to the side. "All you have to do is ask."

Facing my back to him, I turn the music on once more. The new song reminds me of one that would be played at the strip club.

This man is not the only one living a tainted life. There's nothing darker and more degrading than sleeping with men for money. I'm more than used to men seeing me naked.

If this is what he wants, then I will give it to him.

Swaying my hips to the beat of the music, he watches me. I dance seductively, sipping down the rest of the wine before placing my empty glass onto the table.

Running my fingers through my hair, I arch my back, not daring to break our eye contact. Pulling down the top of my dress, I expose my red, lace bra. Reaching around my back, I unhook my bra, and slowly slide the straps down my arms.

Soon enough, my dress and panties pool at my feet. Trying desperately to keep my composure, I stand before him. There's heat in his eyes. Lying beside him on the couch, my legs spread, granting him the perfect view. Every nerve ending is on edge as he watches me eagerly, pushing my fingers through my slick folds.

Closing my eyes, I picture my hands as his own. My skin is scorching. I'm suddenly on fire, aching for him. Pushing a finger into my tightness, I envision it's him, intensifying every sensation. I softly moan, slowly adding in another.

Massaging my breasts at the same time, playing with my puckered nipples, I'm thrown closer to the edge. My fingers are so slippery, and I quicken my pace. I'm squirming before him, moaning, breathing deeply. My stomach tenses, and my legs quiver.

Suddenly, I'm there.

Shattering into a million pieces, I don't even attempt to

hold back my cries, riding out my orgasm until I'm left gasping for air.

My eyes find his. So intense. Flustered, I cover myself with the throw. Without any warning, he stands.

"Fuck," he growls, running his hand through his hair. "You're lucky I'm a man of my word."

And with that, Mr. Edwards dismisses himself from the room.

CHAPTER 7

A few hours later we arrive in California.

The moment I feel the air as we step into the night, I am consumed with euphoria. It's an insane feeling to realize that I get to cross this off my bucket list, traveling to the state of nearly every girl's dream.

The warm air blows my hair in the wind, and my face lights up with joy. Holding out my arms, and spinning in circles, I laugh at how unbelievable this is.

I feel enriched, free-spirited, every emotion enhanced. I take in this very moment, holding it close, because soon enough it will only be a memory.

A beautiful memory.

The runway is lit up just enough to create the perfect amount of light. Breathing in deeply, I smile to myself. Even the scent here is unlike the smell of the city. It's fresh, rejuvenating.

"Wow," I happily say. "It's beautiful here."

My gaze roams over the mountains in the far distance, beneath the dazzling, starry sky.

Glancing over his shoulder, I spot his Ferrari driving down

the ramp from the aircraft. The gentleman who collected our bags steps out from the driver's side, leaving the door agape.

Mr. Edwards opens the passenger side door, and I climb inside. Watching him through the windshield, he exchanges several words with his men, shaking their hands.

We drive down winding roads for what feels like an eternity. Gazing out the opened window, the warm breeze brushes against my skin, and my hair flows freely with the wind.

Arriving at the onset of a driveway, I am blown away. The most beautiful house I've ever seen is right before my eyes. A mansion, to be exact. I am disoriented, entirely speechless. Palm trees are in the front yard in every direction, and there are tall, black lights that enhance the entrance.

We come to an abrupt stop at the top of the hill.

"This is your house?"

"It is," he replies.

Pushing open my door, I rush to my feet, gazing up at the mansion before me in astonishment. Taking in every unique and beautiful detail, a burst of energy overtakes me.

Jaxon closes the door for me, and I quickly turn to face him. Before I can even think it through, I link my arms around him, and rest my face in the crook of his neck.

Smiling ear to ear and bursting into laughter like a little girl, I am enthralled. This is better than I ever could have imagined.

He becomes still, arms motionless by his sides. This is not the reaction I was expecting. Drawing back my head, I look in his eyes, and the strangest feeling settles in the pit of my stomach.

Butterflies.

Stepping back, I sheepishly frown. "Sorry," I whisper.

Right as I turn away, he grabs my wrist and pulls me back into his chest. My heart hammers from our close proximity.

"Don't be," he murmurs.

THE WALLS OPEN BEFORE ME. There's a wide entrance, and a glass chandelier hanging from the tall, gorgeously sculptured ceiling. My heels echo with each step on the polished hardwood floor. I take in the exceptional architecture, the luxurious décor.

A wave of adrenaline comes over me, like the onset of a hurricane. This is far more elegant than I ever would have thought possible. Mr. Edwards strides in a moment later, placing our luggage near the front door.

"Did you say that this is on the beach?" I ask.

"It is."

Unable to contain my excitement, I widely smile. "Can I?"

"Straight ahead, through the sliding glass doors."

Rushing down the hallway and through the dining area, I step out into the night, amazed by my surroundings. There's a rectangular pool, the water a light blue from the moonlight. It's so inviting, tempting me to jump in without even bothering to remove my clothes.

In this moment, I am careless, bringing me back to my childhood, the happy little girl I once was.

There's a large, tall, and dark wooden canopy off to the side. Kicking off my heels as I approach it, I spot a table and chairs. There is a built-in jacuzzi in the fixture. Climbing the steps onto the wooden platform, I'm finally able to see the beach in the near distance.

The darkened waves crash against the shore, and the luminescence from the stars is dreamlike. When I listen closely, I'm able to hear the soothing sound of the water. It's hypnotizing.

"Enjoying the view?" he asks, taking in the sight of me standing in the moonlight. "I know I am."

His hair is tousled from the calm breeze, and his eyes seem

to glisten from the moonlight. The powerful ambiance he gives off makes my pulse quicken. A blush settles on my cheeks, and I force myself to look away.

"This view is amazing. You live such a luxurious life," I say, watching the waves. "You're really lucky."

"I wouldn't say lucky." He gazes out at the ocean, folding his arms across his chest. "Determined, if anything."

"Either way, I wish I could be this happy all the time. If I had your wealth, I know my life would be a whole lot easier."

"Nothing comes easy in life."

"Trust me, I know. My parents died on my eighteenth birthday."

His eyebrows knit together. "I'm sorry."

"I'm over it. Really."

"I can imagine it's not that simple."

"Well, I pretty much lost everything. At that point in my life, I just said fuck it." I laugh, with no humor intended. "Decided to start working at the strip club downtown, and that's where I met Natalie. The worst came after that. Prostituting, I mean."

Shit.

I've said too much already.

"I'm babbling, sorry."

"I don't mind."

"All I know, is that soon enough, I'll have thirty thousand dollars." Releasing a small breath, I grin. "That's more than enough to get me back on my feet. By offering me this deal, Mr. Edwards, you're helping me more than you know."

He remains silent. Stepping closer, he presses his lips into a firm, straight line. Something about the way he's looking at me leaves me weak, unsteady on my feet.

"I take back my original offer," he quietly says. "One hundred thousand."

My heart sinks, and I blink up at him, shocked. "What?"

"You heard me."

"But, why? Why would you do that for me?"

"Why not?"

Like a strike of lightning, determination courses through my entire being. If this man I barely know can do something so selfless, so significant, then why can't I?

"Where's the contract?"

He arches an eyebrow, intrigued. "My pocket."

My, how convenient.

"I'd like to sign it," I announce. "Now."

Jaxon's gaze holds uncertainty. He studies me with a burning desire. Lust, and hunger. Reaching into the pocket of his suit, he retrieves the papers, as well as a pen.

He places them onto the table, and immediately, my attraction to him reaches its highest point. There's no turning back now. I know that I want this. I know that I want him, and he has made it more than apparent that he wants me, too.

"All I have to do is sign?" I ask, slowly approaching him.

He nods. "Sign it, Sasha. Let's make this final. Shall we?"

Without taking another second to think this through, I'm grasping the pen, and signing my full name on the line.

The moment I truly understand what I've just done, I lift my head, and his jaw clenches tight.

"There. It's final."

CHAPTER 8

*T*aking my hand, he leads me to the back door. I can't even remember the last time I craved to feel a man's touch. Until, now.

My body is longing to feel him inside me, to accept every inch he has to offer. My rules and regulations I've had for years as a hooker now cease to exist. They no longer matter.

All that matters, is how badly I need to feel something, anything.

I just want to *feel* again.

The lights in the dining room shine dimly, and I practically melt at my surroundings. The space around us is more spacious than conceivable, and beautifully decorated.

The moment I head toward a doorway, Mr. Edwards pulls me back to him.

"Not yet."

He strides toward the large dining room table filled with expensive décor, and in one swift motion, he swipes it clean. Almost every item falls and breaks against the floor, glass shattering, silverware clinking.

Without warning, he pulls me close and lifts me effortlessly onto the edge of the table. Lifting my arms, he slips my dress over my head, and unclasps my bra. He cups my breasts, his thumbs lightly tracing my hardened nipples.

Arching my back, I softly moan.

"Remove them," he orders, eying my panties.

"Okay."

Sliding them down my legs, my body is now bare. Even though I'm used to being naked in front of men, I have never felt this exposed.

This vulnerable.

"Sir," he corrects me, loosening his tie.

Watching him, keenly, how his fingers quickly undo the knot, I find myself lost in this moment. Paralyzed. When our gazes finally meet, his eyes are sharp.

Menacing.

"Yes," I rush out, lips parted. "Yes, Sir."

He pulls his tie loose through his collar, and places it beside my leg. "Good girl."

Reaching out, I touch his shoulders, feeling the muscle beneath the fabric. Taking my time, tracing his biceps, I carefully guide the jacket of his suit down his arms. They're firm, and his chest is like stone beneath my fingertips.

Grabbing my wrists, he moves my hands back down to my sides.

He unbuttons his long sleeve shirt, and undoes his cuffs one by one, until his upper body is bare. And *holy fuck*, he's beautiful.

My gaze roams from his chiseled chest, down to his toned abdomen, and to the curve at his hips. The impressive bulge beneath his dress pants makes my mouth water.

Within seconds he removes his pants and pulls down his boxers. His manhood springs free, and a feeling of adrenaline overwhelms me. It pumps like nitrous inside my veins, boiling, raging.

Jaxon Edwards is long, thick, and bigger than I could have ever fathomed.

"Turn over," he commands.

Although, I'm unable to move. My stomach tightens, and my breathing is labored. I am completely drenched. I've never wanted a man this badly in my life.

Jaxon flips me onto my stomach. I'm now bent over the table, standing unsteady on my feet.

"When I give you an order, you comply," he grits out, irritated. "You need discipline."

Pressing my palms against the cold surface of the table, I try desperately to catch my breath.

"Chose a safe word."

Jaxon pins my hands behind my back, and there's a feeling of silk against my skin. My wrists are bound by his tie.

He tightens the knot around my wrists, and the fabric digs deeper. "Craving your first punishment so soon, are you?"

"Black," I breathe, squirming against him. "Sir."

"How cliché," he cruelly says, taunting me. "Black, it is."

Wetness pools between my legs at the thought of how powerless I am, tied up and spread out across his expensive dining room table. Knowing he has every ounce of control has my head spinning.

"You've been a bad girl, Sasha."

His palm comes down hard on my ass. Pain claims me, a stinging sensation I'm not quite used to. He gently caresses the tender area, using soft strokes to help ease the discomfort.

"That was one. Count the rest for me."

"Yes, Sir," I shakily say.

His hand comes down again, and the unsettling sting returns. My skin feels like it's on fire. I can hardly wrap my head around the feeling as I tightly shut my eyes.

"Two," I gasp.

The next is much more intense. My breathing hitches, and I cry out, my hands balling up into tight fists.

Holy fuck.

"Three," I whimper, and there's another. "Four."

The last one catches me off guard. My legs begin to tremble, and my knees almost give out. Almost.

"Five," I softly moan, resting my forehead against the cold, flat surface of the table.

"Good girl."

The sound of a foil packet being torn open brings me back to reality. My world spins recklessly. The anticipation drives me to the brink of insanity.

He parts my legs, and lightly brushes my inner thighs with his fingertips. A quiet moan escapes me the moment he eases through my slick folds, and finds my clit. He touches just the right spot, rotating over my sensitive nub in precise circles. My eyes roll shut, and I purr in satisfaction.

"You're so fucking wet," he says, pushing his pelvis against my ass. His large erection rests between my legs, teasing me, toying with me. "Tell me what you want."

"You."

"What was that?" he urges, wrapping my hair around his wrist, and tugging firmly.

I grunt. "I want you, Sir."

Mr. Edwards drives into me with one long, hard stroke. I groan from his invasion, stretching me wide, buried to the hilt. It's deliciously painful. Although I need a moment to adjust, he slams back into me, pressing his fingers into my hips.

"So tight." He smacks my ass, heat radiating beneath his palm. "Do not come unless you are given permission."

"Yes, Sir."

He thrusts harder, deeper, my inner walls tightening around his shaft with each thrust. As I try to pull my arms free from his tie, he holds my wrists, locking me in place.

With each thrust, the table rocks violently. With the sound of skin smacking, and moans filling the room, my pussy is throbbing. He's so fucking big, filling me completely.

Before I'm even able to make sense of it, an intense feeling builds up within me. My stomach quivers, and he kicks my legs open wider.

He grips my ass, and squeezes hard. Thrusting my hips back, he slips his hand to the front of my pussy. My moans echo through the room while he works my clit, pounding into me from behind.

"So close," I whimper, and he slams into me harder. "I'm going to come."

Suddenly, he stills, and his length fills me.

"What did I say?"

"Need your permission," I breathe, my voice husky. "Do I have it?"

"Beg me," he growls, twitching inside of me.

"Please."

"Louder."

"Please let me come, Sir!"

He drives his cock deeper. Forcefully. Urgently. He firmly tugs my hair, pulling my head back. This man fucks me into sweet oblivion, throwing me closer and closer to the edge.

Finally, there's no holding back.

I'm right there.

"Come for me," he demands.

"Yes!"

An earth-shattering orgasm claims me, and I come undone beneath him. My mouth falls open, and I squirm against the table, washed over by waves of pleasure. An explosion erupts through my body, sending me into pure bliss.

This is the first time a man has ever made me come.

He groans, and finds his release with one final thrust. Removing his tie from my wrists, my legs feel like pudding. My heart is fucking pounding. I can't speak. I can't think. I can't even find it in me to move.

In all my life, I've never been fucked like that.

"Turn around," he says.

Attempting to push myself up from the table, it's almost impossible. Jaxon turns me to face him, and lifts me into his arms. He carries me through the house against his chest, and I shut my eyes, giving in to the calm after the storm.

Embracing the soft sheets of a heavenly bed, I sigh with comfort. He drapes the covers over my naked body, and within seconds, I'm overtaken by sleep.

CHAPTER 9

*M*y eyes flutter open, and the beautiful, bright rays of sunshine beam in through my window. Taking in my new surroundings, I finally remember where I am. Sitting upright and stretching out my arms, the sheets fall to my waist.

Quickly covering myself, I come to realize there's no need. I'm the only one in the room.

My room.

With my heart racing, I stand, allowing my gaze to study every detail of the space around me. There's a large, circular window, with peach-colored curtains pulled off to the side.

There's a small balcony beyond the sliding glass doors, surrounded by a white gate. I have the most perfect view of the ocean, twinkling in the daylight.

The walk-in closet has me slip into a state of shock. It's full, equipped with a countless amount of clothes, and even shoes. Dresses, shirts, pants, shorts, comfortable shoes, and even heels. You name it. The options are endless.

It's every girl's dream.

"This can't be for me," I softly say.

"It is."

Jaxon stands in the doorway, silently watching me. He's wearing black dress pants, along with a blue shirt, enhancing those beautiful eyes that somehow seem to hold me captive.

"I always arrange to have new clothing awaiting my Sub's arrival," he explains, folding his arms over his chest. "I want you to feel welcomed here, Sasha."

"Well, you sure do know how to make a woman feel giddy."

He smirks. "You should wear a dress. It suits you well."

"And you should learn how to knock," I counter, and his eyes narrow. *Shit.* "Sorry. Sir."

"Are you?" He moves closer. "The next time I step into this room, you will greet me with respect."

"Yes, Sir."

"Kneel."

Not daring to look away from his eyes, I drop to my knees.

"You are here to satisfy my needs, to serve me," he strictly says, brushing my hair behind my shoulder. "And I've been fantasizing about the feeling of your lips around my cock since the moment you first raised your voice to me."

Watching him unbutton his pants, his member springs free.

"I'm going to fuck that big, naughty mouth of yours."

Looking up at him through my eyelashes, I innocently nod. "Yes, Sir."

He grabs the back of my head, bringing me closer. His fingers are intertwined in my hair, and I don't hesitate for a second. Wrapping my fingers around his manhood, I suck the rosy head of his cock.

Moving slowly, I find just the right rhythm, sliding my lips back and forth over the length of his shaft. Jaxon groans. Pumping him with my mouth and hand, my speed increases.

Without warning, I attempt to take him into the back of

my throat, although it's impossible. Gagging in response, he holds me in the position for several seconds longer.

"Fuck," he sharply exhales.

With his fingers still tangled in my hair, he forces himself deeper, plunging in and out of my mouth.

When suddenly, his cellphone rings.

Removing it from his pocket, he presses the phone to his ear. "Hi, mom," he smoothly answers.

My stomach drops once I remember the other side of this arrangement. Meeting his family.

And here I am, on my knees, with her son's cock in my mouth. He thrusts his hips forward, forcefully, while I grip his waist to keep myself from falling backward.

"Yeah, we had a nice flight," he says, staring down at me with hunger. "Oh, Sasha's doing great."

And he finds his release in the back of my throat.

"Of course," he says, fixing himself in his pants. He leaves the closet, and I rush to my feet, following closely behind him. "Sure. Noon, it is. See you soon. You, too."

And with that, he ends the call.

"We're having lunch with my mom and younger sister. You have less than an hour," Jaxon says, striding toward the door.

Nerves get the best of me.

"So soon?"

"Time to find your game face, Sasha." He turns to me, crookedly grinning. "We're just getting started."

WALKING DOWN THE HALL, I admire the hung paintings on the walls, before arriving at the top of a spiraling staircase. This house is so enchanting. A part of me still believes that this must be a dream.

Placing my hand on the railing, I slowly descend the stairs.

The walls in the living room are maroon colored, with dark, leather furniture, and there's a gorgeous, stone fireplace.

The afternoon light permeates the room, the sun's rays spilling in through the arched, floor-to-ceiling windows, dust particles suspended in air.

"You are hauntingly beautiful," Mr. Edwards says, breaking my thoughts.

He strides toward where I'm standing, and appears to look over every inch of me. My light blue dress matches his shirt, ending several inches above my knees, along with black heels.

When his face is inches from mine, I'm locked in a trance, his handsome features pulling me further and further away from reality.

"Shall we?" he asks.

And I lightly place my hand in his.

THE CAR RIDE to his parent's house is more than nerve-racking, mostly due to the fact I have no idea what to expect. This part of our deal almost seems more difficult than anything else at this point.

Lying truly isn't my specialty, it's the opposite of my tell-it-how-it-is personality. I've never been in love before, and the thought of me having to pretend that I am really makes me anxious.

Nauseated, really.

Standing at his family's front door, I release a small breath. One hundred thousand dollars is on the table. I can't mess this up. I must play the part. The second he wraps his arm around my waist, and brings me closer, my body becomes tense.

"Any second thoughts, Mr. Edwards?"

"Jaxon," he abruptly says, staring straight at the door. "There's no reason to be nervous."

"We're lying to your family."

He smirks. "Fortunately for you, you've never met them."

"Not helping."

His grasp on my waist tightens. "Deep breath, my love."

Suddenly, a woman opens the door with a friendly smile. She has shoulder-length black hair, and bright, blue eyes.

"Hi, mom." Jaxon leans forward, without releasing me, and pecks a kiss on her cheek.

"It's been much too long," she says to him, and without any indication, she pulls me into a warm embrace.

I'm speechless before hugging her back.

"Hi," I nearly croak.

"Hello there." She draws back, smiling with admiration. "I never thought my son would fall in love, or especially become engaged. I am so happy for you both. You are a very, very beautiful girl."

"Okay, mom," Jaxon says, while his mother softly laughs in response. "We're sorry it's taken so long. Work has been brutal over these last few months."

She smiles, exposing her pearly white teeth. "Excuses, excuses."

"I know," he sighs.

"I am your mother and I have missed you." With that, she looks at me once more. "You can call me Lucy."

"It's really nice to finally meet you, Lucy. I'm Sasha."

Tension builds up as she looks us over, admiring the two of us together. Jaxon's grip on my waist becomes snug, and when our eyes meet, he presses a small kiss against my forehead.

"Jaxon!" A young girl's voice takes us by surprise.

Stepping inside, I feel very displaced. The way these people live is far different than the way I've been living, especially for the last few years.

A stunningly beautiful little girl appears in a doorway, sporting a wide smile. Laughter erupts from her as she bolts to where we're standing, wrapping her arms around Jaxon's waist.

"I've missed you!" she exclaims, beaming up at him. "You promised you wouldn't stay away for that long."

"Work has a nasty habit of getting in the way," he says. "I'm sorry. I'll try to not let it happen again."

Her big, blue eyes widen. "Promise?"

"Promise."

It's easy to tell how much she loves her big brother, and it's so touching to watch, until it reminds me that I no longer have a family.

Lucy chuckles, standing beside me. "She adores him," she quietly says. "They have a special bond."

"I can tell."

And I grin, watching them exchange words, practically melting inside. My heart is beyond full.

"Did you get taller?" Jaxon asks her. "You're almost my height."

She rolls her eyes. "Yeah, right. I am not. You're a giant."

"Only six-foot-four," he mumbles.

Her laughter fills the room. "Like I said, giant!"

Turning to Lucy, I grin. "You have two other daughters?"

She nods. "Yes. Debra and Crystal," she explains. "Jaxon is the oldest, while Blake's the youngest."

"And Debra is getting married?"

"Yes." She proudly smiles. "It's going to be a beautiful wedding. Her and Mark, her fiancé, will be returning home from a cruise within the next few weeks."

"That's nice."

"Sweetheart." Jaxon's voice catches me off guard. "This is Blake. Blake, this is Sasha."

She frowns. "I thought you said her name was Louise?"

His face hardens.

Thinking fast, an idea comes to mind. "Some people call

me Louise, my middle name, but I like Sasha better. How about you?"

Blake quietly giggles. "Me, too."

"Thanks," I say, smiling. "I'm so glad to finally meet you, Blake. I've heard so much about you."

"You have?"

"I have."

Meeting Jaxon's gaze, he tucks a loose strand of hair behind my ear. My knees grow weak as he strokes my cheek with his thumb.

"Blake, could you show Sasha to the living area?" Lucy asks. "I'm going to grab some lemonade from the kitchen. Jaxon, will you help me get a few glasses for the four of us?"

"Of course," he replies.

As soon as they're out of sight, Blake takes my hand and leads me into the living room.

She sits on the couch, twirling a strand of her hair around her finger. "I love your dress, Sasha."

Sitting beside her, I grin. "Thank you. I like yours better. Red is my favorite."

"Mine, too!" She drops her attention to my hands on my lap, and appears to be examining something. "Where's your ring?"

Oh, God.

Jaxon and his mother appear through the doorway, carrying a tall pitcher of lemonade along with four glasses.

"Would you like a glass?" Lucy politely asks.

"Yes, please. I'd love some."

"Where is it, Sasha?" Blake repeats her question, holding up my hand to them.

My lips part, and I've become speechless.

"What?" he asks, noticing my uneasiness, and almost over-pouring my lemonade in the process.

"Her ring," Blake dramatically sings, gazing up at him with curiosity. "It's not on her finger."

His jaw clenches tight, and a vein bulges in his neck.

"It's being cleaned," I unthinkingly blurt out. "You know Jaxon, always thinking of others."

He arches an eyebrow at me, intrigued.

Lucy softly chuckles. "Well, isn't he something. He's always had such a big heart."

Oh, Lucy.

That's not the only big thing he has to offer.

AFTER WE EAT a delicious lunch prepared by Lucy, Blake takes me to the dining room. Looking over the framed photos on the wall, I am beside myself. The Edwards family is beyond stunning.

Debra seems to be more around his age, and she's gorgeous. Crystal appears a little younger, and her features are practically identical to Jaxon's. The resemblance between them all is uncanny.

Blake taps my shoulder. "Jaxon was a lot older when I was born," she explains, pointing up to a picture. "That's why he looks so old in some of these pictures with me as a baby."

"I resent that," he retorts, folding his arms across his chest. "Are you implying that I'm an old man?"

"Well, you're not young," she playfully replies. "You're thirty-two!"

Our eyes meet, and he shrugs. "Apparently, I'm old."

"Thirty-two? Hmm. Not so bad."

He winks.

Blake grasps my arm. "How old are you, Sasha?"

"I'm twenty-five. He's seven years older than me," I quietly say, and his gaze lowers to my breasts. I want to smack him for checking me out in front of his little sister, but fortunately, she's oblivious. "Kind of funny, right?"

"Yeah, it is." She laughs, sporting an adorable smile. "I like you, Sasha."

"I like her, too," Jaxon purrs.

"You guys are so cute." Blake backs away from us, and suspicion overtakes her small features. "I'm surprised you guys haven't kissed yet, like Debby and Mark do."

Shooting a nervous stare in his direction, he doesn't look away from his sister for a second. He's become unreadable, still, and way too calm. I for one, am raging with fear.

Lucy steps into the room, and our silence is loud. "Is everything all right in here?" she questions, alarmed.

Jaxon places his hand on the small of my back. "Everything's fine."

"Come on!" Blake urges. "Kiss her already."

"Oh, sweetheart," Lucy sighs. "Don't put your brother and Sasha on the spot like that. It's quite rude."

Blake drops her gaze to the floor, embarrassed. "Sorry."

"Mom, that's absurd. She doesn't need to apologize," Jaxon speaks up. "It's a simple request."

Breathing out a sigh of relief, I'm able to relax. Until suddenly, what he has just said registers in my brain. What could he possibly mean by that? He wants us to kiss? He's okay with this?

No, we can't. We can't do this. I don't want to do this.

Or, do I?

My mind never pondered this moment, not once, and now we are both put entirely on the spot. My face fills with heat. I can tell I'm beat red from the burning sensation beneath my skin. My body stiffens and my senses are heightened.

All I can feel is his hand on my back, and the knot growing in the pit of my stomach. The scent of his cologne washes over me, calming me. When his eyes meet mine, he appears guarded. Conflicted.

Dropping my gaze nervously to the floor, my head is recklessly spinning. My heart is pounding, and my palms are clammy. My knees have grown weaker by the second. This is the moment our no kissing on the mouth rule ends, and it's unsettling.

I haven't kissed a man in years.

Jaxon cups his hand against my face, lightly stroking my cheek with his thumb. It feels incredible to be touched like this by him. So sensual, intimate. He's surely a great actor.

His eyes cautiously search mine as he leans closer, our lips inches apart. He hesitates. It's almost as if he's waiting for permission, or for me to push him away. To stop him.

Although, I remain perfectly still.

Shutting my eyes, I'm ready, giving in to the terrifying, yet sweet temptation, until we're pulled from this moment.

His cellphone rings, and he quickly retrieves it from his pocket. "I need to take this call," he announces. "Business."

And he walks away.

CHAPTER 10

*S*everal hours later, we say our goodbyes. Jaxon requests for me to have dinner ready once he returns home from work, which reminds me of why I'm here. To be his Submissive.

With the sleek granite countertops, stainless steel appliances, and burgundy walls, this kitchen easily puts the one back at my apartment to shame. It's uncluttered, immaculate, and well equipped with everything you could possibly imagine.

There're utensils on hooks, a matching island in the center, along with an empty vase. After exploring his backyard, it's not long before the vase is filled with vivacious, red roses.

The aroma is heavenly, and the light from the sun's rays bring a brightness to every petal. Smiling, I place the vase onto the table, before spotting the mess of glass and silverware on the floor.

My steamy encounter with Jaxon last night immediately comes to mind, having flashbacks of him spanking me, and fucking me into exhaustion.

Shuddering, a cold chill runs down my spine, and I find

myself grasping onto the edge of the table to keep myself upright. Being with him is unlike anything else.

He's handsome, mysterious, powerful.

Dominant.

An overwhelming craving for him settles between my legs. Provoking me. Mocking me. Kneeling on the floor and sweeping up the mess, I try desperately to push every dirty thought of him out of my mind. Although, it's nearly impossible.

I can't quite seem to fight the ache.

NIGHT EVENTUALLY FALLS. We eat dinner in a comfortable silence, although I can tell that something is on his mind. Once we're finished, I clean the kitchen and feel as if there's tension between us.

When I least expect it, Jaxon announces for me to meet him in the living room. The second he disappears through the doorway, I can't help but feel unsettled from the formal tone of his voice. Something is going on.

The quiet sound of music playing is soothing to my ears as I step into the room. Spotting Jaxon sitting on the couch, I make my way toward him.

He gestures for me to take the spot beside him.

"Sit," he says, and it's not a request.

I do as I'm told.

There're several pieces of paper resting on the table, and he holds a pen. Curious as to what these documents could possibly be regarding, I lean forward, allowing myself a better look.

He abruptly turns to me, his eyes beaming into mine.

"Communication is very vital in this relationship," he begins, sliding the papers into my view. "There are safe words, soft limits, hard limits, punishments, and rewards. There're also expectations of both parties, although, I need you to realize that this contract can be terminated at any time."

"Can it?"

"Yes."

I nod in return.

"We've yet to make any changes. If you wish to do so, now would be the appropriate time."

"Changes," I carefully repeat, and my breathing quickens. "I honestly don't know what I would change."

His eyes narrow, and study my face for a moment. "Would you like to reread the contract?"

"I've already read it."

"Then, I'm assuming you're comfortable with all the terms." Placing down the pen, he sits back, resting his arms on the head of the couch. "Do you have any questions for me?"

"Comfortable is a strong word. No disrespect, Jaxon, but this is all new to me. None of this is exactly comfortable."

"Then make the necessary changes where they are due."

"You're paying me one-hundred grand for this. I'm fine with the terms. I can handle it."

Cocking his head to the side, he watches me silently, observing my every move.

"Are you on any form of birth control?" he asks.

"Yes."

"What kind?"

"The pill," I say, chewing on my lip. "And I take it like clockwork."

"Great. I'll arrange for STD testing sometime tomorrow."

"Oh?"

"A blood test."

"Okay. For you, too?"

There's a gleam in his eyes. "Of course," he says.

Listening to the calming melody of the music from the record player, it's not long before my nerves begin to take over.

He leans forward once more, removing another document from a manila folder. "I've printed out another contract."

"For?"

Handing it to me, he stands. "It's a payment agreement, regarding our financial arrangement, legally binding me to my word."

Reading it over, my mouth falls open. "If I'm reading this correctly, then after the six months end, that's when I'll receive the full amount." Releasing a long breath, my heart races. "I wonder how much that is monthly."

"Roughly seventeen-thousand."

My eyes widen, and I shoot him a dazed stare. "Seriously?"

"You get five thousand tomorrow."

"Subtracted from the one-hundred thousand?"

"No," he says, slipping his hands into his pants pockets. "It's a signing bonus."

Wow, what an incredible incentive.

"By check?"

"Cash," he nonchalantly replies. "Sign it."

Without hesitating for another second, I sign my name on the line and date it. After fully understanding how legitimate this is, I am ecstatic, yet utterly terrified of the unknown.

Sensing my distress, he strides across the room, and holds up a bottle. "Whiskey?" he offers.

"No, thanks."

He smirks, pouring the liquor into a glass.

Staring weakly at the bottle, and pushing every erratic thought into the back of my head, I sigh.

"Yeah, actually. Whiskey is fine."

Sitting beside me, he hands me the glass.

Several minutes pass while we sit in silence, the music

playing faintly in the background. When suddenly, a song begins to play. A song I haven't heard in years.

Tears spring to my eyes, and when I turn to look at Jaxon, he's already staring. His eyes are intense, hypnotizing. Quickly looking away, I sip my drink, hoping he hasn't noticed my sudden change.

Although, he has.

"What's the matter?" he asks.

"Memories," I reply, fidgeting with my glass on my lap. "My parents used to play this song all the time. It was played at their wedding." I briefly hesitate. "And, you have a fireplace."

"I do."

"We did, too. They were completely obsessed with that thing. There was always a fire going. Always. And when they died, they left everything in my name, but I just couldn't be there anymore. I left so fast, and I didn't think anything through."

"I'm sorry." Jaxon cups his hand lightly over mine, and I freeze, before pulling away. "I hope you don't mind my asking, but, what happened to them?"

Please, no.

This is not the night I plan to become an emotional wreck.

"Sorry," I whisper. "I can't."

And with that, he nods.

He appears so understanding, sympathetic. Interested, even. It simply has me at a loss for words.

Jaxon stares at me long and hard, intrigued. It's almost impossible to look away. Without warning, he takes my glass and sets it onto the table. Standing, he holds out his hand.

"Dance with me?"

"What?" I ask, taken back by his random gesture.

His eyes are guarded, and his face is now masked. Without hesitating any further, I accept. Bringing us to the center of the room, my mind is racing. It's driving me crazy that I can't even remember the last time I've danced with a man.

Gently placing my hand in his, I place the other over his broad shoulder. Slowly moving along to the rhythm, he holds me closer, his arm snug around my lower back.

Swaying back and forth in a soothing motion, the melody changes. My stomach drops as he dips me backward.

Bringing me back against his chest, I shyly smile. "Well, I have to admit that I wasn't expecting this."

"Are you implying that I'm a good dancer?"

"Not bad, Mr. Edwards."

He crookedly grins.

Jaxon steps back and extends his arm, twirling me around before swiftly pulling my body back to his.

Suddenly, we become still.

The room spins endlessly to the point of no return. My legs become weak, like pudding, and my heart drums wildly as he stares intently into my eyes.

He brings me closer, tightly holding me against him. Standing on tiptoes, my arms find their way around his neck. Slowly leaning down, his lips are mere inches from mine.

Right there.

So close.

Our eyes lock. He clutches the back of my neck, and moves the other to the small of my back. His fingers are intertwined in my hair, and he uses enough pressure to keep me perfectly still. I'm unable to move without pain shooting through the back of my skull.

My heart is fucking pounding. His beautiful, blue orbs stare dangerously into mine. There's so much lust, heat. So much intensity.

He leans down further, our lips inches apart.

And he releases me.

Gasping for air, I stumble backward. Shocked. Confused. What the hell was that?

"I—I'm exhausted," I stammer, breathless. "At least everything went well with your family."

He watches me closely, and his gaze darkens.

"They were really nice."

He turns around, facing his back to me. "Goodnight, Ms. Pierce."

"Goodnight, Mr. Edwards."

CHAPTER 11

*W*aking up to a dark room, I am restless. After tossing and turning for the last several hours, I decide to take a shower. The water is steaming as it trickles down my skin, soothing every tense muscle.

The truth is, I just can't seem to shake away what had happened earlier tonight.

There was a spark between us, undeniable chemistry. Wiping away the mist coating the mirror, I take in the image of me in my black, silk nightgown.

My cheeks are a rosy red from the lingering steam in the room, and my eyes are gleaming with sheer lust. I have an unfulfilled craving, a burning need.

For him. For more.

Descending the spiraling staircase, I don't have the slightest idea on what I'm doing, or what I'm searching for.

Until I see *him*, striding down the dimly lit hallway.

The moment he notices my appearance, he eyes me vigilantly. The shadows enhance every curve and muscle of his chiseled body.

"Sasha," he softly says. "Do you need something?"

"I couldn't sleep."

Taking in the sight of my revealing nightgown, his eyes narrow. There's an intense magnetic field between us, drawing me to him. He looks me over, from my breasts, to the curves at my waist, before setting his mouth in a hard line.

"What do you want?" Jaxon questions me, stepping closer, until my back is forced against the wall.

"Nothing," I whisper.

"What do you want?" he repeats, with authority, demanding honesty. From the ravenous look behind his eyes, I know this is his way of warning me, and I am testing his patience.

I'm on thin ice, pushing his limits.

Begging to be punished.

"You are to answer me when I ask you a question."

The hair stands up on the back of my neck. Lowering my gaze to his bare chest, I defy him.

"No."

Slamming his hands beside both sides of my head, he has me cornered. He pins my arms above my head, locking me in place. Leaning his body against mine, our lips are inches apart. Everything around us begins to spin.

All I can focus on is him.

He releases me, and points to the hardwood floor beneath our feet. "Kneel."

The hard surface is cold against my knees.

"Stay," he commands, turning away.

Watching him silently, he stops near a door, now pointing to the spot before him.

"Crawl."

Unsure if I've heard him correctly, I press my palms against the floor.

"Now," he orders, his strong voice echoing down the hall.

Crawling to him, on my hands and knees, a burst of energy

pulses through my body. I feel powerless, ashamed, yet unquestionably aroused at the same time.

Kneeling before him, he strokes my hair. "Good girl. Now, stand."

Rushing to my feet, he opens the door. We're greeted by darkness. The unknown leaves me terrified. Jaxon walks through the doorway, before gesturing for me to enter behind him.

As I step into the pitch-black room, he turns on the light.

The walls are a dark shade of red, the carpet and ceiling a solid black. There's a faint scent of leather and polish in the air, presenting an erotic, seductive vibe. One wall is full of mirrors, reminding me of a dance studio, and the lighting is dim. Equipment is spread out on racks, and hangs from the walls. There's intimidating gear in what feels like every direction. It's simply endless.

Being in here leaves me with a rush.

Adrenaline.

The chills travel down my spine. This is unfamiliar territory for me, and as unsettled as I am, wetness pools between my legs.

My mind draws a blank once I spot the king-sized bed. He has surely taken his past Subs in here. Cringing, I swallow hard. There's also an X-shaped platform against a wall. What could that possibly be used for? My thoughts begin to race, and my breathing picks up.

The sound of the door closing catches me off guard. There's no escaping this now. There's no escaping him.

He stands close, taking a strand of my damp hair between his fingers. Nervously looking away from his face, my gaze trails down to the sweatpants that are hung low on his hips.

It's apparent that he's in his element as he presses his nose to my hair, breathing in the scent.

"Your hair smells wonderful." He steps back. "Undress."

My nightgown and panties fall soundlessly to the carpet.

Taking in the sight of my naked body, he nods in approval. "Good girl. Get down on your knees for me."

"Yes, Sir."

Immediately, I obey, kneeling on one knee and then the other.

"Tell me who you belong to."

Jaxon walks behind me, until he's completely out of my sight. He circles around me, as if he's a dangerous predator hunting his prey, and in this moment, I am his.

"Now," he sharply commands.

A feeling of warmth washes over me. Leaning forward, I adjust myself on my hands and knees.

"You."

He brings his palm down hard on my ass, an involuntary moan escaping me.

Wrapping my hair around his wrist, he gives a good tug. "Try that again," he cruelly says.

"I belong to you, Sir."

This is Jaxon Edwards behind closed doors. This is his secret lifestyle, and now, it's mine. There is no more wondering about what it will truly be like to be with this man. This is it. This is the start of our six-month relationship as Dominant and Submissive.

"I cannot describe the feeling you've given me. Having you so utterly vulnerable and at my will, it's more than satisfying." He moves around me and leans down to my level. "Close your eyes."

I obey.

Suddenly, the room becomes silent, until I hear a drawer slide open. Without any warning, something soft presses against my eyes, completely blocking out the light.

A blindfold.

"I'm going to bondage you. You will be unable to move on your own. Place your hands behind your back."

Shock settles in and I can't find it in me to move a muscle.

He smacks my ass. "Now," Jaxon growls, impatient.

And I do as I'm told.

My arms and legs are bound, a restraint extending down my back, somehow connecting my wrists and ankles together. It secures them tight, ensuring my head is pulled back.

I am as powerless as one could be.

He lightly traces my nipples, and they harden from his touch. Abruptly, there's a sharp pinching sensation. Inhaling a long, deep breath through my nose, the other side follows. There's a slight tug, and I'm stunned to feel pleasure course through me.

I moan, squirming on my knees.

"Do you want my cock, Sasha?"

"Yes."

"Beg for it."

"Please."

"Louder," he urges.

"Please!"

"No," he denies me. "Not good enough."

"Please, Sir," I loudly moan. "I want you."

"Try again."

"Please, fuck me! Please! I need to feel you buried inside me. Please, Sir."

"Good girl." Something smooth presses against my lips, and up my face, and I finally realize what it is. "This will be yours, soon."

Jaxon pushes me forward until the side of my face is pressed into the carpet. This leaves my ass up in the air, and pulls the restraints tight, leaving me supported on my knees and the side of my face. If only I could see what I looked like in this very moment.

He rubs the tip of his cock against my slick folds, and rotates around, pushing himself up and down the wet slit of my sex. Holding onto my feet, he enters me in one, forceful thrust.

Within seconds he's pounding into me.

Relentlessly.

Showing not even the slightest bit of mercy.

Sinking into me, repeatedly.

The nipple clamps are tugged on, and I moan at the unfamiliar, gratifying feeling. He fucks me harder, smacking me squarely on each ass cheek after each thrust.

My orgasm is building. I am desperate to find my release. I force myself to hold back, which is the hardest thing I've ever had to do.

The smacks on my ass are throwing me closer to the edge. His length strokes my walls, hitting all the right spots. Clenching around him, I relish at the feeling of him claiming me as his.

The space around us is no longer silent. It's now filled with praise and urge as his thrusts grow harder, faster.

"Apologize for your defiance," he commands.

"I'm sorry," I breathlessly say. "I'm sorry, Sir."

"Come for me."

Climaxing hard, my body convulses, and waves of my orgasm consume me. It seems as if it's everlasting. The clamps are pulled off my nipples, throwing me further over the edge. My mind becomes blank, my body is numb, and I'm somehow seeing stars against the blindfold.

"Sasha?"

I remain quiet, paralyzed from the overwhelming feeling of bliss.

"Sasha?" he loudly repeats. "Are you all right?"

Caught up in the feeling of euphoria from my climax, I'm speechless. The blindfold comes off, and the light shines through my eyelids. The restraints are removed next, and I finally regain the strength to open my eyes.

Jaxon kneels before me, firmly grasping my shoulders. I've never seen him look quite so defenseless.

"Are you all right?" he firmly repeats.

"Yes," I faintly say. "I'm okay, Sir."

Taking my face between his hands, his eyes deeply search mine. "Are you sure?"

"I'm fine."

A relieved breath escapes him, and he slightly backs away.

"When I ask you about your mental or physical state, especially when we are in my playroom, you are to answer me immediately. No hesitations."

Remaining silent, completely exhausted, I nod.

He slips his arms beneath my legs and back, and lifts me from the carpet. My body is weak as he carries me over to the bed, laying me gently on my side.

Jaxon climbs in behind me. "My role is to ensure your safety at all times," he says, draping his arm over my chest, holding my tender breasts. "I cannot do that without your communication. Do you understand?"

"Yes, Sir," I quietly reply. "I understand."

He brings me closer, and finally, I'm able to relax in his warm embrace.

Within seconds, everything goes black.

CHAPTER 12

*T*he strangest sensation awakes me. It's as if I'm floating in midair. Jaxon carries me through the house, holding me securely in his arms.

Exhaustion claims me once more, and I drift away.

The sound of a door opening draws me back to this moment. It's clear that he's unaware I'm awake as he lightly places me onto my bed. Shutting my eyes, I pretend to still be asleep, and he drapes the covers over my naked body.

Suddenly, the unthinkable happens.

The warmth of his lips against my forehead leaves me shaken. This sensual act is far different than what I'm used to with this man.

He gently brushes my hair to the side, soothing me. There's a deafening silence in my room. I hold my breath, waiting for the unknown, the inevitable.

Until just as suddenly as this has occurred, he's gone.

Sitting upright, I stare anxiously at my door. What just happened between us?

It was nothing, Sasha.

It meant nothing.

I WAKE up to a gentle knock upon my door the next morning. Sleepily pulling myself out of bed, I open the door to find Jaxon standing in the hallway.

Memories of last night flood through my mind. Disobeying him. Stepping foot into his playroom for the first time. Being fucked into mental and physical exhaustion.

My heart skips a beat.

"Sleep well?" he asks.

I nod.

Cocking his head to the side, his eyes narrow.

"Yes," I quickly speak up, tucking a strand of hair behind my ear. "I slept great."

"Good."

I nod again, and he remains quiet.

Frowning, he folds his arms across his chest. "We need to discuss last night's incident."

My lips part, and I release a shaky breath. "Okay."

"Good," he murmurs, taking in the sight of my naked body. "Dr. Winchester will be here shortly."

My eyes widen. "Doctor?"

"The blood test we spoke about," he says, in a suave tone.

"Oh. Right."

"I'll give you a few minutes."

His gaze wanders to my breasts, and he quickly turns away. Beginning to shut the door, his voice catches me off guard.

"Sasha."

Lifting my head, I freeze, staring into his eyes. "Yeah?"

"Cover up."

Fighting the urge to roll my eyes, I nod. "Yes, Sir."

With that, he disappears down the hall.

Closing the door, I release a small breath, leaning my back against the frame. It's crazy how worked up this man seems to get me. Searching through the closet, I decide on a pair of sweatpants and a comfortable shirt.

Making my way downstairs, the living room is silent, unoccupied. Once I step into the dining room, I spot Jaxon sitting at the table. There's a man standing before him, with his back facing me, and he's just drawn blood from Jaxon.

"Sasha," Jaxon says, and my eyes dart to his. "Just in time." Rolling down his sleeve over the taped gauze, he stands. "This is Dr. Winchester."

It takes him a moment to face me, and when he does, he formally nods. The doctor is an older man, with gray hair, and a stern face. He appears to be all business, and no small talk.

"Good to meet you," Dr. Winchester dryly mutters, gesturing to the empty chair with his gloved hand. "Have a seat."

Glancing over at Jaxon, he nods, reassuringly.

Sitting awkwardly in the chair, I chew on my lip.

"Coffee?"

Looking at Jaxon, I grin. "Please."

And he makes his way into the kitchen.

The doctor removes his gloves and sits in the chair beside me, opening a manila folder. Grabbing the sheet of paper resting inside, he places it before him, and clicks the end of the pen.

"Confirm your name."

"Sasha," I breathe.

He nods once, and scribbles something down on the paper. A moment later, he lifts his head. "And last?"

"Pierce."

"Your age?" he asks.

"Twenty-five."

He scribbles down my answer. "Do you have any diseases?"

I swallow hard, blinking rapidly. "Not that I know of."

He looks up at me again, with a blank face. "Any health conditions?"

"No."

"Have you ever been a drug user?"

"Just for a few years," I joke, although his face remains expressionless. Squirming in my chair, I sigh. "That was a joke."

Jaxon places a cup of coffee in front of me on the table, and shoots me an unimpressed stare. "Answer the question, Sasha."

"No. I've never been a drug user," I smugly answer.

The doctor secures the sheet of paper back into the folder, before drawing several vials of blood from me. After cleaning up his sterile surface, he places the biohazard bags along with the folder into a black briefcase.

He holds out his hand to Jaxon, and they firmly shake.

"The test results should be back by tomorrow," Dr. Winchester explains. "Two days at the most."

"Excellent. Thank you."

"Of course."

Dr. Winchester leaves shortly after, and I can't help becoming nervous at the thought of what he's going to say to me about last night.

Sitting across from me, his eyes lock with mine.

He says nothing.

He just watches me sip my coffee.

Watches me fidgeting with my mug, sliding it back and forth on the table. Blowing on it every so often to cool the temperature, sipping it uncaringly. Watches me nearly burn my lips and tongue in the process.

Watches me squirm uncomfortably in my chair, feeling like I'm damn near about to lose my mind.

The silence is deafening.

Until, finally, I can't bear it anymore.

"You wanted to talk?"

"Yes," he says, his voice low. Tight.

"About last night?"

He nods once.

Releasing an anxious breath, I focus on the steam from the coffee. "I've never experienced anything like that before—"

"—You defied me."

Staring at him from across the table, I frown. "I did."

"On purpose," he adds in. "Why?"

Swallowing hard, I shake my head. "I'm not sure."

"You're lying."

"Am I?"

His eyes turn to slits, and he slowly leans forward, resting his arms on the table. Pressing his hands together, he intertwines his long, lean fingers.

And he shoots me daggers with his eyes.

"You're testing my patience," he grits out, his jaw clenched tight. "I understand this is your first time participating in this kind of relationship, and I'm trying my very best to accommodate your needs as well. Although, I can only control myself for so long."

"Before what?"

"Before I revert to my old ways, who I was *before* you."

My heart pounds, and I can't find it in me to speak.

The thought leaves me terrified.

Intrigued.

Aroused.

So fucking aroused.

"Tell me," he snarls, impatient. "Before you leave me no choice."

"I couldn't wait any longer," I quietly admit. "I needed to see your playroom. I wanted to see what it was like."

"It?" he echoes, brows furrowed. "What *it* was like?"

My breathing hitches, and I blink at him.

And I surrender.

"Being with you," I nearly whisper. "In that way."

He sits back, leaving one hand on the table. Studying my face, he chooses to stay silent. Although, his eyes are urging me to continue.

But I can't.

Because I don't know how to feel about any of this.

I don't know how to feel about *him*.

"And?" he asks, cocking his head to the side. "What are your thoughts?"

My body stiffens, and I dismissively look away.

"Christ," he groans, pushing out his chair and standing. "All right. Fine. We'll do it this way."

Turning my head, our eyes meet.

And it's brutal.

The contrast of his dark hair, brows, and eyelashes, and his ocean blue eyes leaves me disoriented.

Completely off my game.

He presses his palms onto the table, and lets out a sharp breath. "This isn't a goddamn game, Sasha. My responsibility as your Dom is to ensure your safety. Always. Without communication between us, this will never work."

"I understand that."

"Do you?"

"Yes."

"You hesitated last night," he presses. "I asked if you were all right and received no response from you."

"It wasn't intentional."

"No hesitations, or there will be no easing you into this," he says, staring down at me with sharp eyes. "And I'll show you what it's truly like to be with me."

My heart races.

He makes his way to my side, towering over me. "Do I make myself clear?" he asks, lightly stroking my hair.

My stomach quivers as tension fills the room. The air feels electric, and his eyes are piercing.

Warning me to submit. To obey.

So, I do.

"Yes, Sir," I softly say. "You're clear."

"I'll be in meetings all day," he explains, twirling a strand of my hair around his finger. "I've left the number to my driver on the counter if you'd like to get out of the house."

"Thanks," I let out, breathless.

"Your signing bonus is also on the counter."

Oh, *fuck me.*

My heart flutters at the thought of five thousand dollars, in cash. This is worth it. The money makes it all worth it.

Money.

I desperately need the money.

"Thank you," I anxiously breathe, flustered.

"I'm craving to feel your lips," he says in a rough voice, taking my jaw in his hand. Trailing his thumb against my bottom lip, he groans. "Circled around my cock."

Unbuttoning his pants, he pulls them lower, revealing his long, thick, throbbing shaft.

"Get on your knees," he demands.

Although, I don't move an inch, and his face immediately hardens from my lack of listening.

Quickly pushing out of my chair, I drop to my knees. Staring up at him through my eyelashes, my thoughts are in shambles.

I'll show you what it's truly like to be with me.

A part of me wonders.

Another part of me never wants to find out.

Cupping my face with his hands, he gently traces his thumbs against my cheekbones. Lowering one hand to my chin, he uses his thumb to pry open my mouth.

"Suck," he orders, stepping closer.

So close.

My eyes widen as I take in the sight of his straining erection. He firmly holds himself at the base with his forefinger and thumb, the rest of his fingers cupped around his balls.

Opening my mouth further, he guides himself past my lips. It's a tight fit as my lips stretch around his thickness. My mouth opens wider, and I attempt to take him deeper.

"Fuck," he hisses, fisting my hair.

Closing my eyes, I suck harder, cradling my tongue against his length as my lips slide back and forth along his length. A growl escapes him, and he pulls tighter on my hair, matching his hips with my movements.

"Jesus… Christ…"

His cock twitches, and his body shudders.

I moan from the feeling of pain shooting through the back of my head as he pulls harder on my hair.

A roar erupts from his chest.

"You don't have the slightest idea of what I'm fully capable of," he says through clenched teeth, and I lick the tip of his crown, savoring the taste of him. "Fuck… Yes."

Moving my hands from his waist to his member, he swats them away, gripping the back of my head. He thrusts his hips forward, pumping into my mouth.

Harder. Faster.

Air.

I need air.

Gripping his pants, I hold on for dear life, breathing in through my nose to satisfy my deprived lungs.

"Fuck," he bites out, thrusting in farther. "Yes, that's right. Suck my cock as if your life depends on it."

Squeezing my eyes shut, I hold my breath, giving in wholeheartedly. Bobbing my head, meeting his thrusts, gliding my tongue along as many inches as I can handle.

Choking on him. Gagging.

And he finds his release down the back of my throat in long spurts. Finally, he releases his grip on my hair, and steps back.

My tingling lips part as I try to catch my breath, sitting back on my feet. Waiting for his next instruction.

After fixing himself back into his dress pants, he smooths out his tailored, navy blue suit.

And his eyes find mine.

"I should be back before dinner," he says, buttoning his suit jacket. "Have dinner waiting for me on the table."

"Y—yes, Sir," I stammer, watching him carefully as he leaves the room.

Rushing to my feet, I sit back in the chair, taking a sip of coffee to wash away the taste of salt. The sound of the front door closing echoes through the hallways of the house, and I realize I'm alone.

In Jaxon Edward's mansion.

In beautiful California.

With five thousand dollars.

My heart leaps in my chest as I bolt to the kitchen, spotting a white envelope on the counter. Sliding out the large bills halfway, my heart flutters. My breathing becomes erratic.

A wide smile claims my face.

"Shit," I gasp, looking down at the cash in awe.

This is my signing bonus.

And this is just the beginning.

Dancing in the kitchen, and laughing like a little girl, my gaze wanders to the piece of paper with his driver's number.

Sliding it into the envelope as well, I make my way up the spiraling staircase and bolt into my room. Searching through the front of my suitcase, I pull out my cellphone.

Ten missed calls.

Twelve new text messages.

All from Natalie.

Shit.

There's not even two rings before her voice erupts through the speaker.

"Sasha!"

"Hi, Nat," I rush out, stepping out onto the balcony.

"So much for calling me as soon as you landed!"

"I know. I'm so sorry."

"Too busy getting your brains fucked out, I'm assuming?" she sarcastically asks.

I freeze, not knowing how to respond. Confidentiality.

The contract.

"No," I lie, hating myself for it. "Being his personal assistant is no joke. I've been drowning in work."

"Well, that blows."

"My signing bonus makes it all worth it."

"How much?"

"Five grand."

"No fucking way," she squeals, bursting into laughter. "Are you serious?"

Gazing out at the ocean, the wind brushes against my skin, and I've never felt so at peace.

"This is it, Natalie. This is our chance to change. To change everything."

"To change?"

"No more stripping. No more selling our bodies to disgusting, drunk men. This is it."

She gasps through the other end of the receiver, and I can tell that my words hit her hard.

"Sasha… How much are you getting paid for this?"

"We can move. We can go wherever the fuck we want, Nat. We can take that much-needed vacation in the Bahamas like we've always wanted to," I tell her, blinking back tears.

"Holy shit!" she exclaims, her voice cracking. "Really?"

"Yes, really."

"No more prostituting?"

"Never again."

My best friend begins to cry.

And I cry with her.

"We deserve so much more," she mutters, sniffling. "We deserve better than this. You deserve better than this, especially after everything you've been through."

"Do you want me to send you some money?"

"I'm okay," she tells me. "God, I love you."

"I love you, too, Natalie."

OUR TEST RESULTS come back clean the very next day, and before I know it, one week has already passed.

The arrangement between Jaxon and I has slightly changed since our first encounter in the playroom. I've given in completely to the role of being his Submissive.

My determination has been strong, stronger than I ever would have thought possible. The amount of money I'll be entitled to after this contract ends has me on my very best behavior.

Although, I've accepted my new position as his Submissive with ease, tensions have never been higher between us.

The chemistry we have has been more than challenging. It's that magnetic pull I feel when I'm with him, the feeling he gives me when he looks in my eyes.

I just can't seem to shake it off.

Jaxon spends most of his time at work, in meetings, or in his office, while I handle my responsibilities around the house accordingly. Cleaning, cooking, and being ready for whatever he asks of me at his convenience.

It's been a drastic change in my life, although deep down, I know that this will all be worth it.

We have not spent any time with his family, not since the first day I met them. When we get invited out to dinner with his mother, I am ecstatic to get out of the house.

A change of scenery is much needed.

Striding into the kitchen in my red dress, with my matching heels and lipstick, I am confident. I am eager to play my role as Jaxon Edward's fiancée, the love of his life.

When I step further into the room, I happen to spot a black briefcase on the counter. Jaxon turns around, and when he notices my unexpected appearance, there's this look on his face.

I sigh, discouraged. "It's too much, isn't it?"

His fiery eyes meet mine. "No," he vaguely replies.

"Are you sure?"

"Yes."

My cheeks become flushed, and there's a spark in the air. His lips part, and his gaze has never been so profound.

"Then why are you looking at me like that?"

"Because," he says, guarded. "You're strikingly beautiful."

My heart beats wildly, untamed. I sheepishly grin.

"I've booked reservations for a prestigious restaurant downtown. I hope it meets any expectations you may have," he says, zipping open the briefcase, shuffling through several papers. "It's actually my mother's favorite."

"I'm excited."

"She should be here at any minute."

"What are you doing?" I wonder, curious.

He sharply exhales, focused. "Searching for a very important document."

"For what?"

"I have a dinner to attend. A business dinner."

"What?" My eyes widen in dismay. "I thought you were coming to dinner with your mother and I?"

"I had planned on joining, until something important came up."

"And this isn't considered important?" I argue.

"I suppose they're both important."

"No way. Absolutely not."

Finally, he lifts his head, staring blankly at me. "Pardon?"

"You want me to go to dinner with your mother alone?"

"Interesting." A crooked grin plays at his lips. "I had no idea you were the needy type."

"That's not funny."

"You'll be fine. She loves you."

I purse my lips, scowling at him in silence.

His smirk fades, and he looks away. "It's not the end of the world. I can assure you that you'll be fine."

"Oh, wow!" I sarcastically exclaim. "I needed that. Thank you so much for the reassurance."

Within the blink of an eye, he switches to Dom mode. Standing tall, with his chin lifted, and his shoulders pushed back, his demeanor changes. Even though he's in business attire, looking as charming as ever, those eyes are beyond threatening.

Jaxon Edwards is not a force to mess with.

Slowly making his way around the kitchen counter, he approaches me. My breathing quickens from the dominance radiating from him. He moves behind me, and his hand lightly rests against my lower back, trailing lower.

Mocking me. Testing me.

A part of me wants to be thrown over his knee.

"What was that?" Jaxon demands. "I believe I may have heard you wrong."

Releasing a careful breath, I nibble on my bottom lip.

"Do you really want to play this game, Sasha? You know I always win."

"You can't. Your mother will be here any minute," I challenge.

He leans down, his lips beside my ear. "Try me."

Damn him.

"Thank you, Sir," I submissively say, after gathering every ounce of strength that it takes. "For the reservations. Dinner will be great."

His hand lingers over the material of my dress, until he steps in front of me, and lightly strokes my hair.

"That's my good girl."

THE RESTAURANT IS ELEGANT, with its dark walnut tables, marble floors, flickering candles, and live piano music. There are waiters carrying appetizers and beverages around on silver platters. The air is fragranced, and the noise level is high, along with my nerves.

Our waiter turns to Lucy.

"I'll have a glass of Cabernet Sauvignon, thank you," she orders, before returning her attention to the menu.

His gaze meets mine.

"I'll have a beer, thanks."

Lucy lifts her head and gawks at me, impressed.

"Certainly, ma'am," he dully responds. "Would you prefer anything specific?"

"It doesn't matter." Hesitating, he appears confused. Fidgeting with the menu, I sigh under my breath. "Corona. Thanks."

"Of course."

With that, he scurries away.

To my surprise, Lucy chuckles. "I haven't had a beer in ages," she admits. "Jaxon's father got me hooked on wine."

I grin. "I think Jaxon is trying to get me hooked on whiskey."

"I don't know how anyone can tolerate that God-awful taste."

"Me, either."

We laugh.

"You know, Sasha, pardon me for being so frank," Lucy pauses briefly. "But, I wasn't sure if this day would ever come."

Blinking at her, unsure with her statement, I say nothing.

"My only son falling in love. Proposing," she finishes, and she looks so relieved, so honored. "I've been worried about him. We all have. He's always been quite a loner."

"Has he?" I ask, interested.

She nods. "Most certainly. And nobody deserves to be alone in this world," she says. "Especially not my boy. He has a great heart."

"He does."

"I can tell you love him."

My stomach drops, and I can't find it in me to speak a word.

"The way you look at him," she continues. "It's the way your face lights up. There's a glimmer in your eyes."

Staring at her silently from across the table, I frown, stunned.

"Really?"

"Yes." She smiles. "When he had first told me about you, and about the engagement, I've never been so pleased. I'm so happy for the two of you, Sasha."

Playing the part, I fake a smile. "Me, too."

She sighs. "It's really too bad Jaxon couldn't make it tonight."

"I agree. I've never met anyone more invested in work."

"Ah, yes. He's been that way for many years."

"Has he?"

She nods, perusing the menu. "He has, especially after he graduated from college and started his first business."

"Jaxon Enterprises," I guess.

"Yes. He moved to Chicago and we hardly ever saw him. He's extremely business oriented. His father's the same way."

"What does he do?" I ask.

"He works at a law firm as an attorney."

"Wow. That's incredible."

"Yes, although, it surely does take up a lot of his time." She chuckles. "We had first met while he was in law school. I honestly don't know how he did it. Nursing school was hard enough, but becoming a lawyer," she murmurs, shaking her head. "I could never."

"Me, either."

We laugh, and our waiter returns with our drinks.

"Ready to order?" he formally asks.

"Oh, jeez. We've been talking up a storm," Lucy replies. "Can we please have a few more minutes?"

"Certainly."

And he dismisses himself from the table.

"Can I ask you something, Sasha?"

Meeting her careful eyes, I'm struck with nerves. "Of course."

"How did the two of you meet?"

Thank God.

"At a café," I answer, relieved we had come up with a cliché backstory in advance. "I had accidentally left my wallet at home and was almost turned away, until Jaxon offered to pay."

She happily grins, sipping her wine.

"We ended up sitting with one another, and we talked for over an hour."

"How sweet," she encourages, smiling. "Which café?"

I flinch. *Shit.* Fortunately, I think fast.

"Nellie's Café, in downtown New York."

"Sounds very quaint. Is that where you lived at the time?"

"Yes." I anxiously sip my beer. "Born and raised."

She nods. "Do your parents still live there?"

My heart immediately drops. "Um, no," I dryly mumble, dropping my gaze to the flickering candle in the center of our table. "They passed away."

"Oh, goodness," she gasps. "I am so sorry, Sasha."

"It's okay," I reassure her, forcing a grin. "You didn't know. They died when I was eighteen."

Suddenly, she reaches across the table, and rests her hand over mine. Lifting my head, my glistening eyes meet hers.

"I'm so, very sorry for your loss," Lucy emotionally says, squeezing my hand. "I cannot imagine the pain you went through."

"It was difficult. It's still difficult," I admit.

"The more you talk about it, the easier it will get. Time heals all wounds."

"That's what they say."

"I know we've only just met the other day, but I want you to know that I am here for you. We are all here for you."

A knot forms in my stomach from her sincerity.

"Thank you," I murmur.

"Of course. After all, you're a part of our family."

Family.

The room spins. My body tenses, and my breathing becomes uneven. Guilt consumes me, knowing that deep down, this kind woman has no idea. I'm not a part of her family. I never will be.

This is all just a lie.

SHUTTING the front door behind me, my thoughts have never

been more erratic. There's a heaviness in my chest, and I can't quite seem to catch my breath.

Walking across the living room, I stop abruptly in the middle, gripping the couch to keep myself steady. A soft melody is playing through the record player, and it only seems to make me feel worse.

Much worse.

That unsettling feeling becomes stronger, building inside me, until it's screaming at me. The atmosphere feels dense. It's as if my whole world has been thrown off, pushed off track, and nothing seems to make sense anymore.

In my logical mind, I know that I shouldn't feel this way. I should be happy, ecstatic about this arrangement between us.

Ecstatic about the money.

Although, everything has somehow changed in the matter of an hour. Guilt blazes inside of me, a burning frenzy of doubt, sadness, and fear. After having dinner with Lucy, his wonderful mother, this deal doesn't seem as appealing as it once was. Lying, I can get by with, but under these new circumstances, it just feels wrong.

Lucy made me realize that for this past week, my feelings have grown more than I ever would have expected.

For the money, for his family.

For *him*.

I've been falling deep and deeper into this world, his world, and that's the thing. This world belongs to him, not to me. The only thing I'll be entitled to at the end of this arrangement is one hundred thousand dollars, and I'm not so sure if this is worth it anymore.

I've allowed myself to *feel*, something I haven't done in years, and I'm terrified of the outcome. I am terrified of losing something important to me again.

I'm terrified of losing myself.

"Sasha," Jaxon announces, pulling me from my thoughts. "I didn't hear you come in."

Instead of turning to face him, I stand still.

Silent.

"When did you get back?"

Finally breathing, I turn on my heel, and my eyes dart to his.

There's such intensity. Passion. A glimmer in his beautiful, blue irises that I can never get enough of.

He steps closer.

"About a minute ago," I softly reply.

Cocking his head to the side, he studies my face, before stopping dead in his tracks. "What happened?" he asks, demanding.

"Nothing happened."

"You have this look." He scowls. "Something's wrong."

"What look?"

"Don't," he sharply warns, moving toward me. "Do not act as if you don't know what I'm talking about."

I stare at him, trying desperately to keep my composure.

His eyes narrow, and turn dark. "Does she know?"

"Know, what?"

He towers over me, and his gaze is piercing. "Have you fucked up at dinner?"

"No," I snarl, offended. "Dinner went fine. Your mother is fine."

"And, you?"

I'm completely fucked up. About *this*. About *us*.

About *you*.

"I'm fine."

"Oh, Sasha," he breathes, lightly stroking my cheek with his thumb. "You know where dishonesty gets you. Or, perhaps, I could remind you?"

Quickly stepping back, his hand falls from my face, and he appears alarmed.

"What the fuck is going on with you?" he snaps.

"I can't."

"You can't, what?" he urges, striding toward me. I move behind the couch, putting it between us. "Sasha?"

"I can't," I repeat, breathless. Confused. Powerless.

Jaxon stares silently at me, horrified. He remains motionless, quiet, as I pace back and forth across the room.

"Dinner went great, Jaxon. Your mother is a complete sweetheart. She is caring, thoughtful, and kind. She speaks so highly of you. She cares about you so much."

He nods. "Okay. And?"

I stop pacing. "She's so happy that you've found someone."

"And?"

"You didn't find someone," I unthinkingly blurt out. "It's all a lie, and I'm a part of it."

"I don't understand."

"I really thought I could do it," I tell him. "Until she told me that I'm a part of your family now, and it just hit me."

"What are you trying to say?" he asks, enraged, making his way across the room as I silence the record player.

"You and your damn soft melodies."

"Are you done?" he growls, eyes wide.

"Done?"

"With us?"

Looking up at him, I sneer. "Are we breaking up?"

"Give it up. Tell me what you want." He moves closer, his face mere inches from mine. "Tell me what you want, Sasha, and I'll give it to you. Anything. Anything you fucking want. Tell me."

His deep, soothing voice makes me weak. Time seems to stop and a hurricane of emotions sweep through me. The feeling this man gives me leaves me helpless, so helpless it has me questioning everything. Going from living as a prostitute, who makes the rules, to a Submissive, who obeys the rules, has been a huge challenge for me. This is not me, and I'm tired of pretending that I'm okay with this.

This last week has been much more than I had bargained for. It's been a battle of not allowing this experience to change who I am, how I am, and I don't know if I can do this anymore.

"I want to leave," I murmur.

His face instantly softens, and his lips part. "Don't."

As soon as I begin to turn away, his fingers lock around my wrist, and he pulls me against his chest.

"You can't."

"Of course, I can," I argue, glaring up at him. "You even said so yourself. This contract can be terminated at any time."

He grimaces, loosening his grasp on my wrist, as I draw back my arm. "This is it, then?" Jaxon stares angrily into my eyes. "You're leaving because of guilt?"

I hold my breath, disordered.

"Great," he huffs. "Un-fucking-believable."

"Will you stop swearing at me?"

He laughs, running his hand through his hair. "I'm angry."

"Well, that makes two of us. You brought me into this mess."

"Don't you dare," he snaps, defensive. "You gave me your consent. I didn't force you to sign your name. You wanted this. You were begging for this."

"Begging?" I repeat, laughing from frustration. "I was not begging."

"You jumped at this opportunity, Sasha."

"Do I look like I'm still jumping?"

His eyes turn to slits, and he folds his arms across his chest. "You do understand, that by you terminating our contract, you're still going to be hurting my mother, correct?"

My heart sinks.

He's right.

"I'm starting to realize that you hardly ever put yourself first."

I frown. "What is that supposed to mean?"

He steps back, shaking his head in disappointment.

"Well?" I urge him.

"You're being well compensated for this arrangement. This isn't all for nothing. You were in a shit place, and I gave you a way out. A golden fucking ticket."

"And what, the money is supposed to make everything okay?"

"Sure, it is!"

"Like hell," I retort. "You billionaires are ridiculous. Happiness can't be bought. You aren't the one without a family."

"Oh," he softly says. "That's what this is about."

"Don't give me that."

"Give you what?"

"I don't need your pity," I angrily breathe, pointing my finger against his chest.

His eyes flicker sincerity, the opposite of what I was expecting. "I would never pity you. I understand."

He grabs my wrist, and stares deeply into my eyes.

I quickly step back, distancing myself. "You weren't the one with your mother at dinner. You have no idea how I feel about any of this. Don't act like you do."

He laughs, with no humor intended. "Is that so?"

"I need some space."

"No."

"You don't own me, Jaxon."

He groans, grabbing my arm, tightly holding my bicep. "Don't you fucking get it?"

Trying to break free from his grasp, I glare at him. "Get what?"

"I care about you." Jaxon swiftly pulls me back to him, lifting my chin with his finger, ensuring complete and total eye contact. I practically melt beneath his touch. "Stay with me, Sasha."

My breaths become uneven, and my stomach quivers. His tongue traces his bottom lip, and oh, *fuck*, his lips look so soft.

Shit.

"Oh, you're good," I slyly say, pulling away from him. "Reverse psychology."

"Bullshit."

I wave my hand at him dismissively. "I'm calling a taxi."

"Fine. At least allow me to arrange for my driver to escort you."

Turning on my heel, I stride out of the living room, and hurry down the hall. Reaching the front door, he takes my wrist again, and pulls me back to him.

"Jaxon—"

"Here." He places the key to his Ferrari in my hand.

"Why?"

"To ensure you'll come back to me."

Without exchanging another glance, I take back my pride, and step into the night.

Somehow, I manage to take advantage and stay out for over an hour, driving around aimlessly. After all, I'm on the other side of the country. I have no friends here, and surely no family.

Not having the slightest clue on where to go to ease my mind, I settle on the beach just a few miles away.

There's a calming light from the moon illuminating the waves as they crash violently against the shore. It's as if they're reading my mind, and feeling my turmoil, how lost I've become.

I've never felt so alone.

AFTER ARRIVING BACK to Mr. Edward's house, my head is still spinning, and I feel so out of place. Pushing open the front door, I make my way inside, and the dull silence has my heart accelerating.

My heels click against the wooden floor in the living room, and Jaxon is nowhere in sight.

Unexpectedly, I'm grabbed from behind and pushed up against the wall. Taking in the heat behind Jaxon's eyes, something has changed. The intensity of his stare has me captivated, dazed. Struggling against his chest, he holds me tighter.

"What are you doing?"

"I'm not sure," he breathes.

And his lips crush against mine.

CHAPTER 13

*B*efore I can even make sense of it, I'm kissing him back with urgency. I've never been kissed like this before. It feels like a surging tide of warmth, the opening of my soul. My body feels as if it's levitating off the floor, and I'm floating in midair. Fireworks are exploding, bursting into millions of pieces right at the brink of our lips.

Nothing else exists.

Nothing else matters.

Jaxon groans, bringing me closer, and every inch of my body dissolves against his. I breathe in his heady cologne, shampoo, and aftershave, everything that makes him, *him*.

He grabs the back of my neck, and presses his fingertips into my skin. I am enraptured at how good this feels, how right this feels.

His arms circle around me, forcing me closer, and I'm on fire against his touch.

Our lips part, and he lightly cups my face with his hand. "Don't leave."

My lips quiver, and he stares passionately into my eyes. Gently brushing my cheek with his thumb, he leans closer.

"Stay with me."

How could I not?

And he presses his lips to mine once more. Tilting his head, he deepens the kiss, tracing his hand down my spine. Jaxon emits dominance, firmly massaging my tongue with his. I cling to him, as if he's the only solid thing in my world.

Jaxon scoops his arm under my legs, lifting me from the floor, as he walks us across the room. Placing my body onto the couch, he hovers over me.

Kissing his face, I trail my lips across his jaw, planting small pecks against the slight stubble on his neck. He groans, low in his throat, while I trace my fingers along his muscular arms.

"Fuck," he breathes, pulling off his shirt.

He removes my clothes, and my heels. After unzipping his pants, he rolls me onto my belly. Parting my legs, Jaxon sinks into me.

Kissing my shoulder, he thrusts hard. He pins my hands behind my back, holding my wrists together, pushing into me over and over.

Gripping my waist, he pulls me back, until I'm on my hands and knees.

"My favorite fucking view," he growls, spanking my ass. "I'm going to ruin you. No other man will fill you the way I do."

He enters me hard, and I grunt, pushed forward from the force. My inner walls tighten around his thick cock with each thrust. My orgasm rapidly builds up as he fucks me relentlessly, pounding into me like a wild animal.

Wrapping my hair around his wrist, he pulls hard, gripping my shoulder with his other hand to secure me in place.

There's the sound of skin smacking, uneven breaths, and urgent moans. My mouth opens, and I'm gasping, desperate for air to fill my lungs.

"Come for me," he orders.

My eyes roll back, and my toes curl. Aftershocks of my climax consume me. He pushes me flat on my stomach, and I'm left whimpering, panting. Trembling beneath his masculine body.

"That's right. Take my cock," he says through clenched teeth. "Take all of it."

Pulling tighter on my hair, he gently bites my shoulder, and slows. With deep, merciless strokes, he finds his release. Rolling onto my side, he lies beside me. Breathless, sweaty. Lips parted, eyes filled with darkness.

Mystery.

I can't figure this man out for the life of me.

He lightly traces patterns against my shoulder blade with the tip of his finger, and finally, his eyes meet mine.

"What are you doing to me, Sasha?"

Leaning closer, his lips brush against mine. My eyes flutter shut, and I fist his hair, losing myself in him. Pulling him closer. He kisses me longingly, moaning under his breath, gripping the back of my neck to hold me still.

Jaxon rolls over, pinning me beneath him. He presses my hands into the leather couch, eagerly exploring my mouth. His body is strong, heavy, and it's a struggle to breathe.

Although, I care more about the feeling of his lips against mine than I do about air.

"We need to get away from here," he says against my lips. "From all of this."

"Where?"

"So eager," he purrs, smirking.

He abruptly stands, and I take in the sight of his glorious body.

Oh, fuck.

He's so handsome. So daunting, primitive.

"You'll find out in the morning," he says, holding out his hand. "Get to bed."

"Yes, Sir," I mutter, placing my hand in his.

WHEN I AWAKE the next morning, I feel giddy. That's an understatement. It's like I'm a child again, waking up on Christmas morning, ready to run down the stairs to open my most desired presents.

A suitcase rests in the hall outside my bedroom door. After packing a few outfits, I realize that he must be taking me somewhere that we will be staying for at least a night or two.

But where?

Once I've showered, dressed, and I've finished packing my bag, I finally arrive in the living room. He's nowhere in sight. The moment I step foot into the kitchen, my heart nearly stops.

Jaxon has prepared an incredible breakfast. The full plates are spread out on the dining room table, and he's drinking a cup of coffee while reading the newspaper.

No man has ever cooked me breakfast before. Who knew that Jaxon Edwards could be a gentleman?

"Good morning," he says, eying me from across the room.

Staring at him in awe, he smirks, and gestures for me to take a seat. Pancakes, bacon, and omelets. The aroma can't even compare to how delicious this breakfast is once I take the first bite.

"This is incredible," I say, smiling. "To die for."

He nods, sipping his coffee. "Good."

"Do you enjoy cooking?" I ask, taking another bite.

"On some occasions. I hardly cook for just myself."

"Well, not trying to boost your ego or anything, but these omelets are the best I've ever had."

He grins.

"So, where are we going?" I ask.

"It's a surprise."

I frown, sighing. "I hate surprises."

He shrugs as I pour myself a cup of coffee.

"Well, you're wearing a suit. We're going somewhere fancy, I'm presuming?"

"I'll be changing soon," he tells me. "I was at work this morning. I had to ensure a few things were taken care of before we left."

I arch an eyebrow. "You work a lot."

"Eat your breakfast."

As soon as we've finished eating, he carries our bags to the car. Looking over his attire, I'm stunned to see him in dark jeans, a casual black shirt enhancing his biceps, along with bulky boots.

Looking down at my heels, I mentally scold myself.

"You'll be needing sneakers," he says, breaking me from my thoughts.

I unzip the suitcase which rests in the trunk, and retrieve the pair I've packed from back at home.

"Are we going hiking?" I question, kicking off my heels.

"No."

"Are we taking your jet?"

"No," he says.

And we hop into the car.

Two hours pass, and suddenly, our surroundings change. We're driving down long, quiet streets, and woods surround us. We pass by lakes and farms, such beautiful scenery, throwing me even further off guard. The excitement is unreal.

"This is beautiful!" I exclaim, happily gazing out the window at the fenced-in horses.

"It is."

Closing my eyes, I relax in my seat, adoring how drastically everything has changed.

"We're here," Jaxon announces.

Immediately sitting up, I watch as he takes a sharp turn

and begins to drive down a curvy driveway. Right when I least expect it, the trees open before us, and I stare at the sight before me in astonishment. There is a large, beautiful log cabin.

Now this is what I call a romantic getaway.

Stepping inside the cabin, my new surroundings have me elated, astounded by the beauty. There're wooden walls, polished hardwood floors, and tall wooden pillars. There's a large, stone fireplace in the living area and a wall entirely made up of glass.

Trees are grouped together in silent formation, mountains far out in the distance. There're tall bushes, flowers, and weeds out beyond the windows, and there's not one cloud in the sky on this gorgeous day.

My gaze roams over the ceiling, taking in the beams and beautifully sculpted structures. The wall of logs creates a rustic feel, with the smell of cedar and the cozy, warm feeling it sends over me. Sunshine lights up the room, rays beaming in through the glass and illuminating the floating dust particles in the air.

Jaxon shows me out back as we step onto the deck, down the few flights of stairs, until we reach the concrete area. An outdoor table along with chairs is off to the side, along with a fire pit built into the ground.

Gazing out in the distance, there are tall mountains and hundreds of miles of trees. Looking up, I take in the sky's beauty, listening to the sounds of nature.

"I'd like to show you something," Jaxon abruptly says, holding out his hand. "Come."

"Okay," I say, and place my hand in his.

We make our way toward an open path in the woods,

enhanced with pebbles in the ground. Walking down the trail hand in hand with Jaxon feels surreal.

Everything between us has changed so drastically, it almost seems to be a dream.

"I have to be honest," I break the silence, hesitating. "I didn't think you knew how to have fun."

"Is that so?"

"Well, yeah. You're always just so obsessed with work."

"It's not an obsession," he presses. "It's my career."

"If you say so. I haven't done anything fun like this in a long time. It's been all about working my ass off and trying to make enough money to pay the rent on time." Suddenly, a thought hits me. "Shit. Natalie. My portion of the rent."

"It's already been taken care off," he tells me. "The night I met you, you said you were having a bad night at work—"

"I don't want to talk about it."

"Where exactly was work?" he wonders, dismissing my words as I gently pull my hand from his. My cheeks fill with warmth. How embarrassing to discuss my personal life with a man who has done so well for himself. "Was I right, Sasha?"

"Yeah," I bleakly reply. "I worked at the strip club. Not the proudest highlight of my life, but it did pay the bills."

"I apologize. I didn't mean to intrude."

"It's fine, really. I'm just not used to sharing it with anyone."

His eyes carefully search mine. "You shouldn't have to."

"Natalie and I first just worked as strippers," I begin to explain, my gaze roaming along the trees. "But then money still somehow managed to get tough. Living in the city probably wasn't the best idea. So, we decided that we could make a little extra, selling a little extra."

"You'll never sell your body to another man again."

"You're right. I won't."

We walk forward, suddenly approaching what seems to be

the very end of the path. Now on the edge of the land, almost a cliff, there's a lake down below us.

The water is shimmering from the brightness of the day, the sun's hot rays penetrating my skin. This lake must go out for miles, and there's a countless number of trees surrounding it. It's mesmerizing.

"Wow." My smile becomes so wide, my cheeks begin to ache. "You're kidding me."

"Can you swim?" He asks, catching me off guard.

"Yes," I reply, staring at him with wonder. "You want to go swimming next?"

"How about now?"

"No way."

Jaxon scoops me into his arms, and I squeal with excitement. He pushes off the edge and we hit the warm water. I come up gasping for air, exhilarated, laughing as I stay afloat.

And without thinking it through, I splash him right in the face. Screaming and trying my best to swim away, he grabs me by my waist under the water and pulls me to him. As soon as my giggles fade away, I look in his beautiful eyes and everything changes.

"I aim to corrupt you," he murmurs, planting a firm kiss on my lips. "In the most beautifully, sinful way."

"Whose am I, Mr. Edwards?"

"Mine," he growls, kissing me once more, exploring my mouth. Feverishly, endlessly. "You are mine."

Jaxon trails soft, torturous kisses down my jaw, sucking on the delicate flesh on my neck below my ear as I drown in satisfaction.

Pulling away, I belt out a laugh. "Cramp!"

"Where?"

"My foot!"

He laughs, his flawless smile sparkling in the sun's rays. "Can you make it back to the cabin?"

"I hope so," I playfully reply, until he pulls me onto his back.

"Hold on to me," he seductively says, as I link my arms over his broad shoulders and around his neck. "Don't let go."

I could never.

Once we arrive to the back of the cabin, we reach land. Stumbling out of the water in our now drenched clothes, laughing like school kids, we tightly lock hands. He helps me out of the lake and pulls me to my feet, and our eyes lock. Jaxon stares down at me with a look of passion, want, need. His lips part, and it's clear he's trying to contain his composure until I simply can't fathom the heat in his eyes.

My body crashes against his. Our lips collide, and his tongue invades my mouth. Kissing him back with everything in me, his hands trail over my body, bringing me closer.

"Now," he breathes into our kiss. "I need to be inside you, now."

"Now?"

"Right here." He strips me until I'm naked. "Fuck."

I pull his shirt over his head, gazing up at his God-like body with admiration. His biceps are flexing and his toned chest is firm against my palms. I trace my fingertips over his sculptured abdomen, trembling as I reach his belt.

Jaxon tosses his pants onto the grass and we move onto the ground. Taking my wrists between his hand, he presses them against the ground over my head, holding me captive. Squirming against his body, he rubs the tip of his cock against my slick folds, sending my sensitive bundle of nerves into overload.

I'm on fire, aching for him.

"Please," I moan, as he plants small kisses against my jaw.

"Please, what, Sasha?" he demands an answer.

"Please, I want you."

He slowly eases into me, inch by inch, until his length is

filling me. Attempting to accommodate his size, he stretches me, buried to the hilt. He stills, before easing out and thrusting forward.

"Yes," I cry out, his grip on my wrists tightening. "Jaxon."

My legs open wider on their own accord, allowing more of him, until he's consuming me. Each thrust is deliberate, slow. Suddenly his pace quickens, pushing into my core forcefully.

He releases my hands, and I wrap my arms around his back, feeling his muscles flex with each movement.

"I was made to be inside you," he breathes, staring longingly into my eyes. "I can't get enough."

His length strokes my walls, and his warm lips find my neck. Sucking, nibbling. It's a beautiful torment I can never seem to get enough of.

Reaching between my thighs, he firmly rubs my clit, and my legs shake violently.

"Don't stop," I plead, digging my nails into his back.

He groans, sinking into me harder. Ruthlessly, until my orgasm is right there.

And he sees it in my eyes.

"Let go," he orders. "Come for me."

With one long, quick stroke, my climax finds me. I cry out to him, waves of extreme pleasure bursting through my body. My breathing nearly stops as I'm overwhelmed by this life-shattering feeling. It's unimaginable.

Although, he doesn't stop.

He continues to move inside me, my inner walls tightening around his shaft. Jaxon groans with each thrust, pumping into me like a wild animal. Trailing his lips to my exposed chest, his warm lips circle around my nipple, the tip of his tongue flicking against my hardened bud.

"Oh, Jax," I cry out, and another wave of my orgasm overtakes me.

He reaches down my body again, lightly tracing his fingers

against my swollen clit, sending me to the brink of the edge. Every part of me begins to convulse, giving in to the sweet, barely tolerable sensations.

I desperately try to hold myself together, although it's no use. I fall into pieces, shattering beneath him.

"Fuck," he growls, resting his forehead in the crook of my neck. "I'm going to come for you, Sasha."

And a moment later, he swiftly pulls out, releasing himself onto my belly.

Falling onto his side, we're left gasping for air. The sun's hot rays enhance the ocean blue color of his eyes. They beam straight into my soul to the point where I'm enraptured, captivated.

A feeling creeps up on me, a feeling I've never felt before for any man. Oh, hell. So intense, so terrifying.

So right.

"Let's stay here forever."

He looks out at the water. "I haven't come here in years."

"It's beautiful, out in the middle of nowhere. You have so much privacy. How could you ever leave this place?"

"It doesn't fit well in my life. Not with my work ethic, at least."

"That's actually kind of sad."

Our eyes meet, and he appears confused. "Sad?"

"Yes," I carefully reply. "Sad. It's sad that your job takes up so much of your time. Time is precious. I've learned that."

"I've dedicated most of my life to building a stable career, and building a name for myself as well. I'm genuinely okay with where I am today. I've worked very hard for this."

"For beautiful houses left unoccupied for years," I chime in. His face hardens. "You know, you could just sell it. I'm sure a family would love to own something so gorgeous."

"I don't need the money."

"That's not the point," I say with a laugh. He rolls his eyes. "Never mind."

"Don't never mind me," he sarcastically mumbles. "Finish. Finish what you were about to say."

"Okay," I slowly begin, hesitating for a moment. After searching for the right words, finally it comes to me. "This seems like the perfect house to start a family. To be married, and to have children."

He remains quiet, almost startled from the guarded look behind his gaze.

"Not implying that you need to get married and have kids, but, you know what I mean—"

"I know," he speaks over me. "Is that what you want?"

My heart flutters. "What?" I nearly whisper.

"Is that what you would like?" He quietly asks. "To get married and have a family?"

It dawns on me that I never really thought about it.

"Well, I don't know." My throat becomes dry, my voice cracking. "Isn't that what any woman would want?"

"You're not just any woman, Sasha."

My heart begins to pound in my chest. "No?"

"You're far, far from that."

"Jax," I breathe, so many emotions flooding through me. His eyes widen as I lightly brush my fingertips against his cheek. "Thank you."

I search his eyes, contemplating my next question.

"And what do you want, Jax?"

"It's much more humid than I had anticipated." He stands, disregarding my question, holding out his hand as he brings me to my feet as well. "Let's wash off."

Just like that, he walks out into the water.

CHAPTER 14

*I*t's the pure blackness blanketing the sky that makes the moon so beautiful. My soul feels serene as we have a candlelit dinner beneath the stars, feeling whole again from the tranquility of this moment.

With every breath comes exuberance, a calming peace as I listen to the sound of the crickets chirping, and the rustling of the leaves on the trees, and the howling of the wind.

The flames of the candles flicker and move with the breeze, as I cut into my filet mignon.

"This is heaven," I quietly say, more to myself than to him. "I thought I loved the city, but it doesn't even compare to this."

"I'm glad you're happy here, Sasha."

"Have a lot of your Subs come here?"

Sipping my wine, there's an eerie silence, and I observe him closely. The orange glow from the flames of the candles illuminates his masculine features, enhancing his strong jawline, dark brows, and his sharp, mysterious eyes.

He stares at me intently, his irises gleaming in the moonlight. "You're the only woman I've brought here," he says, guarded.

My breathing hitches. "Oh."

"You're hardly drinking your wine."

Glancing down to my nearly full glass, I shyly grin. "I guess I'm craving a beer tonight."

He arches an eyebrow, impressed. "I'll grab you one," he mutters, dismissing himself from the table.

Once he disappears through the back door, I'm finally able to release the deep breath I've been holding in for several minutes. It's a bizarre feeling to realize that I'm the only Submissive he's brought to this cabin. That must mean something.

He returns with an ice-cold bottle of beer, and sets it down beside my plate. "All you had to do was ask."

After nearly chugging down half the bottle, I let out a satisfied sigh. Suddenly, something dawns on me, and my shoulders become tense. It's a thought that hasn't even crossed my mind, not until this very moment.

"There it is," Jaxon says, pouring another glass of Bourbon. "You have that look."

"No, I don't."

His expression becomes unreadable. "Look where being dishonest has got us."

"It got us here," I counter, taking another bite.

He sighs. "Honesty remains in the contract."

There is the answer to my question.

I look him straight in the eyes. "So, the contract still stands."

He slightly frowns, cocking his head to the side. "Of course, it does, Sasha. Why wouldn't it?"

And he's right. How could I think it would be any different?

LAUGHING SO HARD my stomach hurts, on the living room floor, I place my empty beer bottle onto the table. I haven't had this much fun in years.

"That's the funniest story I've heard in a while," I drunkenly giggle. "I needed that laugh."

"It's not funny. More embarrassing than anything," he retorts, chuckling himself.

"You're laughing, too, so it must be funny."

He smirks, leaning forward to pour another glass of whiskey. "I'm only laughing because your laughter is contagious."

"Tell me another. Please?"

"No," he states, stretching his arm out over the head of the couch. "It's your turn."

"You want me to tell you a funny story now?"

"Anything," he swiftly answers. "Tell me anything."

"Hmm." I hesitate, trying to think of a childhood memory. "My dad used to take me to Disney World without my mom knowing. She would sometimes have to travel for work. It would only be for a few days at a time, but whenever she would leave, he'd dismiss me from school and we would drive down to Florida."

He grins. "That's a nice memory."

"One year, I didn't tell my parents what I really wanted for Christmas. When I didn't get the gift, I wrote a letter to Santa, and I called him a fat bastard."

Jaxon laughs, smiling wide. "That's gold."

"I always wondered about my parent's reaction to that."

"Probably the same as ours."

Laughing, I lie back, gazing up at the ceiling in deep thought. My parents were the most loving, caring, and compassionate people in the world. They always put me first and made sure I had the best life possible. I haven't talked about them in years.

My smile fades.

"Sasha?" Jaxon asks, pulling me from my thoughts. "Did you hear anything I just said?"

"No," I murmur. "I'm sorry."

"Were you thinking about what happened to your parents?" He asks, and my heart sinks. Once I turn to catch his eyes, he immediately frowns. "I'm sorry, Sasha. I forgot."

"I was eighteen."

Finally, I'm ready.

"Are you certain?" Jaxon interrupts me, eyes narrowed. "I don't know if this is a good idea. You shouldn't push yourself."

Dropping my gaze to my lap, I can feel the tension in the room. A part of me is pleading to myself to not dare speak a word about what had happened to my parents. Then again, there's another part inside of me which is begging to finally let this out.

"We've been drinking."

"It's okay," I reassure him. "I'm okay."

"Wait." He sits beside me on the floor, and gently holds my hand. "Look at me."

His eyes pool attentively into mine, and the second I'm about to look away, he lightly cups my face. "You don't have to do this."

"I want to, Jax."

He nods.

"It was my eighteenth birthday. I went to school just like any other day, and everyone was planning a birthday party for me later that night. My friends were so excited and I obviously was too. I could finally say that I was an adult, you know? Officially eighteen.

"I got home that day and my mom was her usual happy self, and my dad had just got home from work. Everything was going great. My mother took me to the mall and bought me this beautiful red dress. It was gorgeous, and I was so excited to wear it to the party.

"Then, the night came around. I was all dressed and ready." I hesitate and immediately look away from his intense stare, no longer able to speak.

"You can stop there," Jaxon urges, tears springing to my eyes. "You don't need to finish the story, Sasha. There's no reason for you to relive it tonight."

"My mom came into my room and told me that they had dinner reservations at my favorite restaurant that we went to every year for my birthday. I was so mad. That one year I wanted it to be different. I just wanted it to be different, since I was finally eighteen, you know?"

"Of course."

"When I told her about the party my friends planned for me, she got really hurt. I hurt her feelings because going to Olive Garden every birthday of mine was a tradition, probably because I was an only child. We were such a close family. We loved each other so much, we really did."

There's silence, and I begin shaking. Jaxon holds my hand tighter.

"I told her for just once I wanted to go to this party with my friends, that I hoped she understood, but she wouldn't take no for an answer. She was being unreasonable. She didn't even care about what I wanted to do for my own birthday. Wow, I sound like a terrible person. I swear I wasn't a bad daughter."

A tear falls, and he brings me closer to him. "You weren't a bad daughter, Sasha. You were a teenager and you wanted to be with your friends."

"I got so mad that I said some really mean things. I was so disappointed and angry that she wanted to go out to dinner so bad. I told her that I hated her. When we got in the car, I gave them both the silent treatment. I wasn't answering either of them. I remember her turning around and asking me why I was being so mean to her—" I force myself to stop, no longer able to hold back my sobs.

Bursting into tears, I break down. I cry to him. I cry harder than I had ever thought possible. I haven't talked to anyone about this, not ever, nobody other than the police officers and kind nurses at the hospital. Letting this out after so many years is such a horrible, yet relieving feeling. Jaxon pulls me onto his lap and rests me sideways, holding me close, while I rest my forehead against his shoulder.

"Stop," he urges, although I continue to sob. "That's enough."

"I was arguing with her and my father got upset, so he turned around to look at me, until all the sudden this big truck came at us out of nowhere." I gasp for air. "All I remember was seeing their faces and the bright light from the truck's headlights before we flipped over. Jaxon, I woke up on the side of the road all alone. The last thing I saw was our car, and oh, it was so bad. There was blood everywhere."

Sobbing, our eyes meet, and there're tears running down his face.

"Don't cry. Please, don't cry," he says, nearly begging me, tightly squeezing his arms around my body. I press my face into his chest and he holds the back of my head.

"I was so mean to them, Jaxon. It was all my fault."

"No," he sternly says, whispering into my ear. "It wasn't."

"If my father didn't turn around and tell me to stop being so horrible to my mom, then maybe he would have seen the truck coming at us. Maybe there never would have been an accident. Maybe, then, they wouldn't have been crushed in the car," I whimper, my heart pounding wildly as flashbacks of the wreck flow through my mind. "My mom was calling out to me. I heard her. I heard her calling my name. Until she went silent, and I never heard her voice again."

"Jesus, Sasha," he says, holding onto me for dear life.

"It was my fault, Jax."

"No, it wasn't. It was an accident. It wasn't anyone's fault. Things like this just happen, and although they're terrible, and heart-wrenching, nobody is to blame. You aren't to blame, Sasha."

I sob. "They're dead because of me."

"No, they're not."

Jaxon tries to soothe me, but his words aren't convincing. He gently rubs the back of my head, and I can't stop crying. Breaking. Hurting. Slightly rocking me back and forth on his lap, he wipes away my tears with his thumb.

"I told them I hated them," I cry out. "My heart aches for them. It's a burden I'll never get rid of."

"I'm sorry," Jaxon whispers. "I'm so sorry."

Jaxon lifts me, carrying me bridal style across the house. We enter his bedroom, which is off-limits to me, and he places me on the bed. He strips down to his boxers, turns off the light, and sinks into the space beside me. Covering both of us with the silky sheets and comforter, he wraps his arm around me, our legs tangled together.

I rest my cheek against his bare chest, enjoying the warmth that radiates beneath his skin, while he runs his fingers through my hair.

Tears still manage to leak from the corners of my eyes without my permission, as I silently listen to the sound of his heartbeat.

Minutes must pass by and all I can hear is the sound of our uneven breaths, and even though I just went through an unimaginable amount of pain from telling my story, deep down I feel relieved.

"I'm here, Sasha," he quietly says, meaning it deeply. "I'm here."

CHAPTER 15

The moment I awake, the sight of a bird captures my undivided attention. It rests on a branch beside the large, glass window.

The innocence of this moment has me at peace, taking in the beautiful scene of nature before me.

Watching him silently, he turns to face me, slightly tilting his head. He's covered with elegant, royal blue feathers. It's a blue jay, my father's favorite bird, and for a split second it has me wondering.

Could it be?

Could my father be visiting me in the afterlife, represented as his favorite bird, the morning after I finally spoke about my parent's death? The shivers travel down my spine, the mere thought leaving me in a state of bliss.

Closure, almost.

And it lifts its wings, effortlessly flying off into the sky.

Turning over onto my side, the sight of Jaxon catches me off guard. He's innocently sleeping beside me, and I've never seen him look quite so peaceful.

The way the sun's rays lighten his hair, his relaxed lips, and long, dark eyelashes; he is simply beautiful.

This man has slept with me all night, breaking one of his biggest rules yet.

Not wanting this touching moment to end, I drape his arm over my waist, and he pulls me closer in his sleep. His body heat sends a sensation of warmth through me. It feels sensational.

Pressing my face in the crook of his neck, I breathe in the heady, lingering after scent of his cologne. There is no place else I'd rather be than in his arms, protected, and safe. Snuggling into his firm body, it's not long until sleep welcomes me once more.

Awaking, my eyes sleepily flutter open. His spot in the bed is vacant, and I am alone. I turn over and lay on my back, glancing around the room to see if I can spot him anywhere.

He is nowhere in sight.

The moment I step through the doorway to the living room, the brightness is entrancing. Through the glass wall, the sun beams in, creating a heavenly scene before me.

The sky is crystal blue, very few clouds anywhere in sight, and the mountains out in the distance have me in a state of serenity. I could surely get used to this life.

Suddenly, a figure appears from the corner of my eye.

Jaxon is standing in the doorway, quietly observing me. This man has captured a part of my heart and I know I must have captured a part of his. Today, I find myself happy to be alive. I made it out of my traumatic past alive, and maybe now is the time for me to let it go and move on.

I deserve to be happy and I deserve to be loved. I don't want to punish myself for another minute. Since releasing my deepest feelings, and having Jaxon comfort me and tell me everything will be okay, I know that everything will be all right.

A small blush crosses my cheeks. "Morning, Jax."

"Good morning." His tone comes out edgy as I approach him. "Sleep well?"

"Yes, very." Taking his shirt between my fingers, I stand on my tiptoes and softly kiss his lips. The second my eyes open, I'm taken back by the discomfort on his face. "What?"

"Sasha," he says, stepping back.

Swallowing the lump in the back of my throat, something inside is warning me that this isn't right. The way he's staring into my eyes is different. Something has changed. My heart drops into my stomach as I grasp it, hoping I won't fall apart.

"We should talk."

"Alright," I nearly whisper.

"I can't do this."

These words slip out of his mouth with ease, cutting me like a knife. My mouth falls open and just as I'm about to respond, he continues.

"I don't like what we're doing here. We're playing games, toying with one another. It's brutal, really. This is not a real relationship. This is a binding contract, a deal. This isn't me. This isn't who I am, Sasha. I don't understand why I let it go this far. For that, I apologize."

"What?" I ask, now glaring. "Who you are? What are you talking about?"

"I'm sorry." He frowns. "Did I not make myself clear?"

"Jaxon," I say, forcing a smile. "Come on. Don't be like this."

Once more, linking my arms around his neck, I press my lips against his. Running my fingers through his disheveled dark hair, he snakes his arm around my back, and then lightly pries me away from him.

I blink up at him, stunned.

"Please, don't." His brows furrow, and he exhales a sharp breath, pinching the bridge of his nose between his fingers. "Just stop, Sasha."

"What?" I croak, my heart sinking deeper. Stepping back, I hold my breath.

"Don't make this any more difficult than it has to be. It's redundant."

My face beams red, hot. "After all day yesterday, the fun we had together, and dinner under the stars, you're telling me none of that mattered to you?" I ask, astounded. "I told you what happened to my parents. I never told that to anyone—"

"Enough." He shakes his head. "I'm done, Sasha. I'm telling you what's going on right now. You need to stop speaking while I tell you exactly what is going to happen from this moment forward—"

"You are going to tell me what's going to happen," I repeat his words, anger consuming me as I force a laugh. "Fuck you!"

"Is that really necessary?"

I remain silent.

"Our deal was that you would pose as my fiancée to my family, and become my Submissive behind closed doors, and you agreed to that. One hundred thousand dollars is on the table right now. My contract did not imply nor state anywhere that we would kiss and sleep in the same bed. You never suggested that you wanted it to be this way between us. That was not part of our deal," he calmly says, as I stare up at him in disbelief. "Feelings and emotions weren't a part of our arrangement. I'm finished with that. Do you understand me?"

His eyes stare dangerously into mine, empty, unreadable.

"No, I don't."

Jaxon steps closer, breaking any bit of distance between us, our faces mere inches away. "I cannot and will not change who I am for any woman, Sasha, not even for you."

All the color drains from my face.

"You're my fake fiancée the moments we are with my family. You are my Submissive and *only* my Submissive while I am your Dom any moments we are behind closed doors. That is all we are to each other. You'll be a good little girl and comply with the rules of the contract, and I will do my part. If you can't wrap your head around these conditions, then our arrangement is over."

My heart hammers forcefully. I can feel it hard in my chest.

"Meaning, I don't get the money, and I go back home."

"Yes," he responds. "I will put our documents through the shredder, place you on my jet, and fly you back to New York. And I will never contact you again."

Tears threaten my eyes. I fight against them. The pain must be written all over my face, yet his gaze remains cold.

"Tell me what you're thinking, Sasha."

"I'm thinking about how I possibly could have seen any good in you, when in all honesty, you have no good in you."

His jaw clenches tight, twitching, and anger flickers in his eyes. "Yes or no?"

"You need me to pose as your wife-to-be. Don't act like you don't."

"You cheated."

I gawk up at him, uncertain. "What?"

"All I have to say is that I broke off our engagement, because I caught you in bed with another man." He straightens his posture and I emotionally gasp.

"You wouldn't."

"Oh, but I would."

His innocent family flashes to my mind, the sight of his heartbroken mother and sisters. I would never in a million years want to do that to any of them, and I can't even fathom that he would be okay with doing something so horrible.

"You're awful," I whisper, looking away.

"I never intended for this to happen. I want everything to go back to when we first met, although I know that's surely not possible."

I shake my head. "You're right. It's not."

"I still want you," he says, moving closer as I move back. "I care for you, Sasha, just not in the way you'd like me to. I've been living this lifestyle for years and this is what I want. This is what I need. It doesn't mean that I don't still crave you, or want you."

"I can't."

His eyes narrow, and he seems shocked. "You can't? So, our deal is off?"

"I don't know."

All this time of not wanting to be his Submissive, and to possibly become something more, I never really expected to fall for this man the way I did. The truth is, I care about him more than I've cared about anyone else in my life, and no matter how terrifying it is I just can't help but want him in that way.

I've never been the kind of girl who depended on anyone else, especially on a man, but from the moment we met I've felt such a strong connection between us. I thought he felt something for me, too, but I was wrong.

Even though this is the last thing I want to do, to lower myself down to this level, I know that I'm in desperate need of this money. I have come this far and I am not willing to back down at this point in my life. I am stronger than that.

"Okay," I murmur under my breath. "Fine."

He walks forward, his intimidating eyes piercing through mine. "Say it."

"Yes."

"Yes, what?"

Immediately, I correct myself. "Yes, Sir. I agree to these terms."

"No." He slowly shakes his head, lightly caressing my jaw. "Address me as Master."

Inhaling an anxious breath, I attempt to hide my disgust. "Yes, Master," I nearly choke out, hating how it sounds coming from my mouth.

This is the true Jaxon Edwards, and he will change for nobody. Not even for me.

"Forget every kiss we shared, Ms. Pierce." His eyes darken, and he lightly runs his thumb against my lips. "They will never happen again. Understood?"

Swallowing hard, I nod. "Yes, Master. I understand."

"I do care about you, Sasha. You understand that, don't you?"

"No, Master." My eyes meet his, and my knees grow weak. "You don't care about me, and that's fine. The least you could do is be honest about it. Show me the same respect."

"Oh, Sasha." Jaxon holds the back of my head, brushing my hair with his hand, twirling his fingers through the long strands. "I'm sorry you feel that way, truly, I am. Although, don't act as if you didn't know what you were getting yourself into.

"You know how I am, that I am a Dominant, and that this is the only kind of relationship I participate in. I don't want to hurt you any further. That is why I gave you the option to leave."

"I need the money," I carefully say, eyes fixated on his. "That's the only reason I'm still standing here with you. Otherwise, I would have already left."

"Kneel, on the floor, on your hands and knees."

His command takes me by surprise at first, until I come to realize that I have no other choice than to do as I'm told. If I don't, I'll be punished, and I'm not ready for that just yet. Kneeling on the hardwood floor, on my hands and knees, I am determined.

"Good girl," he breathes, finally back in his element. "Why can't you always be this great of a Submissive? It gives me such an indescribable pleasure when you obey."

Why can't I always be a great Submissive to him?

Well, I guess that is all I'll ever truly be to him. Nothing more.

At this moment, I know that the only possible way I'll be able to get through this is to put a stop to the madness, to end these feelings.

Shutting my eyes, I let them go.

CHAPTER 16

*H*atred comes toward me at the speed of a bullet, and I have been triggered. My heart feels as if it's been ripped from my chest and stomped on. I feel used, betrayed, and disgusted. Mortified.

I've allowed my guard to come down with this man, and in return he has turned on me. I've never been so disappointed in myself in my twenty-five years in this world. I can't believe I was naïve enough to fall for everything he was saying. Words. They were just words to him.

They meant nothing.

I'm only here for one reason from this day forward, and that's one-hundred thousand dollars. That's more money than I could ever receive, especially from working as a stripper. This money will save me, give me a new outlook on life, and I can start over from scratch.

Now, I completely give up with disobeying Mr. Edwards. Emotions no longer exist for me as I push them into the very back of my head, building up an unbreakable wall.

From this very second until our contract ends, I will be one thing to him and one thing only.

His perfect Submissive.

"Open your eyes," he orders, in a silky voice.

Immediately obeying his command, I now see him in a much different light. He's not the man I had been with yesterday. Kneeling inches away, Mr. Edwards concentrates on my face, as if he's attempting to read my thoughts.

I swallow hard. "Yes, Master."

"In order for this to work, I need to have your trust. All of it, as much as you can possibly give—"

Right away, I speak over him. "I don't trust you," I softly say. "Sir."

"Pardon?" he lets out with a rumble.

"I confided in you. I told you about what happened with my parents. You lied to me, you betrayed me. You ruined that trust. You made it very clear that you no longer care about me anymore, and for that, I can't trust you."

His eyebrows knit together and he stares into my eyes, intrigued.

"Master," I quickly add in.

"I assumed I had already made it clear that I care for you. If I didn't care, then you would no longer be here with me. As my Submissive, I will take care of you. I will ensure you feel as safe and secure as you possibly can. This could be a very great experience for you, Sasha, if you weren't so against giving it a damn try."

"Yes, Master."

"Come," he announces, holding out his hand. "I'm taking you to the shower."

Accepting it, reluctantly, we walk through the cabin hand in hand. My thoughts are erratic. My world is spinning. I feel lost.

Stepping into his room, my mind is on overload. My senses are heightened. I feel as though I don't belong anywhere anymore, and it's devastating. How stupid of me to let him in so easily.

The master bathroom is extraordinary. Although, before I have the chance to look over my surroundings, his image catches my attention from the corner of my eye. Jaxon unlocks our hands, steps out of his shoes, and our eyes meet.

"Take off your clothes for me," he quietly purrs.

The seduction has me crawling out of my skin. My body defies my mind as my stomach clenches, quivering, and my nipples harden. Longing for his touch.

"Slowly."

Ever so carefully, I obey, taking my time pulling my shirt over my head. It falls to the tile floor silently. His gaze roams over my chest. My pulse quickens. Without wasting another second, I reach around the back of my bra and unclasp it, before sliding it down my arms.

The top of my body is now entirely bare, exposed for him, and the hunger and need he has for me is astounding. Even though I assumed it would make me feel sick to my stomach after what he has just done to me, it doesn't.

I don't feel any emotions at all, just sheer emptiness. Jaxon's gaze trails back to my blank face. Before he can give me another order, I grip the hem of my shorts.

My movements are slow, and torturous, as I slide them down my thighs. They trail past my knees, down my legs, and finally they're pooled on the tile beside my feet.

"You're so beautiful," he breathes. "Undress me, Sasha."

He leans the back of his waist against the counter of the sink. Grasping the bottom of his shirt, I pull it up his torso and over his head, dropping it to the floor. Staring at his toned upper chest, I find myself breathless. My gaze wanders down his sculptured abdomen, to the V-shape curved at his hips.

Jaxon rests his hands on the counter behind him and glances

down to his erection covered by his sweatpants. Kneeling on my knees, the cold tile presses against my skin, and my fingertips lightly graze the hem. Carefully pulling them down, along with his boxers, his member springs free. So thick, long, and big.

How can a man this perfect, have such a horrible soul?

My heart aches.

Before I can make another movement, he takes my arm and helps me to my feet. My gaze catches the mirror behind him, and I take in the sight of his muscular back and firm butt. I softly sigh.

Watching as he steps into the incredibly large walk-in shower, he turns on the water. Steam fills the space around us. Once he meets my uncertain gaze, he motions with his hand for me to join him. After entering the shower, I can't help but watch his backside as he stands under the water.

Suddenly, he turns to face me. My body tenses as he moves me beneath the showerhead. Taking in the sensational feeling of the warmth, goosebumps rise on my skin from the mixture of the hot water and cold air.

Without any warning, I feel his body press against my back. His arms wrap around my waist, holding me close as his hands cup my breasts. This is the first time I've showered with a man. This realization leaves me shaking. My stomach quivers with a longing desire.

I can't fight it.

"Do you want me?" he grits out.

I can't deny it as my body betrays me. "Yes, Master."

He massages my breasts, twirling his fingers around my puckered nipples. A soft moan escapes me. His other hand caresses me, trailing down my belly until he presses his fingers through my folds.

I'm on fire against him as his lips find my neck, sucking gently on my skin. I bite my lip between my teeth, trying desperately to silence myself as he rubs my clit in slow, torturous circles.

Jaxon dips his finger inside me, and my back arches. He adds in another, curling them, gently stroking my walls. My breathing quickens as he thrusts harder, his thumb rubbing my clit at the same time.

"Please," I whimper, moving my hips to match his pace.

"Please, what, Sasha?"

"Please, fuck me."

He withdraws his fingers from my wetness. "Lean forward and stick that incredible ass of yours out for me."

I press my palms against the wall of the shower.

"Good girl," he bites out, smacking my ass. "I want to spank you raw."

"Do it," I encourage him, begging for the slightest bit of pain. "Please, Master."

"You want me to spank you?"

"Yes, Master."

Smack. My skin stings, suddenly feeling hot. *Smack.* The burning takes me by surprise, lingering. Not easing. *Smack.* My flesh must be red, as he moves to a new spot each time, minutes passing by as pain unexpectedly engulfs me. There it is. The pain I've been searching for, yearning for. *Smack.* Harder, much harder. Intensity overwhelms me, as tears threaten the corners of my eyes. So much force. So much pressure. *Smack.*

"You drive me fucking crazy," he growls, over my whimpers.

He enters me in one fast, smooth motion. Thrusting hard, pounding into me. This time, it's different.

It's forceful, emotionless. Rough. Although that's what makes this more satisfying, the mere fact that there are no longer any emotions attached.

It matches me perfectly, since now, I feel empty.

His grip on my hips tightens. Time passes by until my

climax is rapidly approaching me, and I'm pushed closer and closer.

His strokes are quick, deep, brutally possessive. My legs begin to tremble, my knees grow weak as I try not to slip.

Suddenly, I'm right on the brink of the edge.

"Not yet," he commands, almost reading my thoughts.

He turns me around and sits on the bench of the shower, and pulls me onto his lap.

"Ride my cock, Sasha."

Slowly, I sit back on his shaft, accepting him inch by inch until he's filling me. Consuming and stretching me. He links his arms around my back and brings me closer, holding the back of my neck to secure me. Bouncing up and down on his member, I find the perfect rhythm, quickening my pace with his every groan.

He leans forward and takes my nipple into his warm mouth. My fingers run through his disheveled, wet hair until he traps both of my wrists behind my back, holding them hostage.

"Come, now," he growls, grazing his teeth against my shoulder.

My breathing hitches, and my head falls back. An unimaginable orgasm settles in my core, as I continue to move, feeling myself tightening around him. Squeezing him. Leaning into him, I'm consumed with pleasure, listening to the sound of his sharp breaths until finally, I'm able to breathe again.

Coming back to reality, still on Mr. Edward's lap, our eyes lock. He does not say a single word.

Rushing to my feet, the hot water beads down my skin as I shut my eyes. The wall in my head stands strong. I will never be the same.

His voice interrupts my thoughts. "Allow me."

Noticing the soapy sponge in his hands, he moves behind me and washes my back. My shoulders and back tense on their own accord, as he brushes my hair over the front of my shoulder. My mind draws a blank after realizing the intimacy of this moment.

"Would you?" he asks.

Turning to face him, I nod. He turns his back to me, as I take in his masculine appearance, hating myself for still being so attracted to him.

Pressing the sponge against his shoulders, the suds spread on his smooth skin, and there's an eerie silence between us.

Jaxon hands me a towel and I wrap it around my body, and he wraps his around his hips. Without saying a word, he leaves the bathroom. Following behind him, I hesitate in the doorway. He must feel my gaze as he suddenly turns to shoot me an unreadable stare.

"Yes, Sasha?"

"Can I go to my room now?" I softly ask.

There's a subtle change in his expression.

"Yes," he vacantly answers. "You may."

With a small nod, my gaze drops to the floor. I head further into his room, ensuring to keep distance between us as I walk past him. As soon as I reach the door and turn to face him once more, he's frowning.

My gaze travels over to his bed as I think back to how we had just slept in it last night, together, and how I woke up with him beside me this morning. He was holding me so tight, so close.

I felt so safe in his arms.

Jaxon was beautiful. I trusted him and believed every word he said, and I fell for his charming ways and lies. I thought he was being honest with me. I had so much fun with him, fun I haven't had in years. Most importantly, I had finally broken down and I told him my story. I confided in him and he comforted me. He made me feel safe. Jaxon made me happy.

Now, I'm far from that. I'm lost. I'm broken. All I want to do is be alone right now.

In a monotone voice I say, "Thank you, Master."

Watching his face drop as I leave his room, I close the door quietly behind me.

THE NEXT DAY COMES QUICKLY, and we make it to Jaxon's parent's house at around eleven o'clock in the morning. He had explained to me that today I'll be meeting another one of his sisters.

It's safe to say that I am completely on edge. A part of me wonders if we will still be able to pull this off, this fake engagement, especially with how I feel about him now. Some of me hates him, although another part of me understands.

This was our deal from the start, and I intend to play my role as best as I can.

Blake opens the door with an innocent smile. "Hey, guys!"

"Hi, Blake," I happily reply, accepting a tight hug.

"I love your dress!" she exclaims, shifting her gaze over to Jaxon, appearing confused. "Why are you in a suit?"

"I have a meeting after brunch," he replies, an edginess in his tone.

"Grumpy." She crinkles her nose at him, before taking my hand. "Are you hungry, Sasha?"

"Starving."

"Crystal has been dying to meet you," Blake explains, nearly dragging me into the house. "Crystal! They're here!"

Several seconds later, she appears.

With her dark, wavy hair, and her bright, blue eyes, she appears to be Jaxon's twin.

"Hi," she happily says. "You must be Sasha."

"I am. It's so nice to finally meet you."

"I've heard very much about you," Crystal says, laughing. "Blake is a huge fan of the two of you."

"Hey," Jaxon murmurs, giving Crystal a one-handed hug. "How have you been?"

"Pretty good. I've been really busy with school lately."

"Nursing school, right?"

"Yes." Crystal dramatically sighs. "It's complete hell."

"I want to be a business owner," Blake announces, sneaking a look up at Jaxon. "I want to live in huge houses, too."

"It's very time consuming," I speak up for him. "He works all the time. That's why he barely knows how to have fun." Gazing over to him, his jaw clenches tight. "Isn't that right, sweetheart?"

"Hardly," he smugly answers, faking a loving smile. "That's why we went up to the cabin yesterday and jumped into the lake together in our clothes and shoes, right?"

My heart sinks at the memory.

"Aw," Crystal sighs, smiling at Jaxon. "That's so romantic. I didn't think you had a romantic bone in your body."

"Hilarious," he mumbles, sneaking his arm around my waist. It's much closer than my liking. "Candlelit dinners under the stars, you name it. I'm full of romance."

Unthinkingly, I step away, and his arm falls to his side. My eyes widen once I realize what I have done. All eyes are on me.

Especially Jaxon's.

His eyes flash me a silent warning. "What's wrong, baby?"

"I'm fine."

"Are you guys in a fight?" Blake asks, her lips quivering. "Is that why you guys won't kiss?"

Crystal looks in our direction, eying us curiously. "Well, maybe they just don't like to make out in front of people, Blake. Some couples don't like PDA. Did you ever think of that?"

"What's PDA?" Blake asks.

"Physical display of affection," Crystal informs her. "Some people would rather not suck face in front of others."

Tension fills the room.

Swallowing hard, I force a smile. "We're not like that."

"Most certainly not," Jaxon agrees. "Although, once we start kissing, you can never get us to stop. Right, Sash?"

He pulls me close and leans down, pressing a soft, lingering kiss against my lips. My heart hammers and my stomach turns. I was not prepared for this. Jaxon promised that we would never kiss again.

He wraps his arm around my waist and holds me closer to his body, and everything begins to spin far beyond my control.

Suddenly, this moment truly registers in my brain. This man has the audacity to kiss me, after he destroyed me.

How dare him.

Immediately pulling away, our lips part, and I bolt out of the room.

CHAPTER 17

*A*drenaline courses through me, pumping nitrous through my veins. My heart begins pounding, my body trembles, and I find it nearly impossible to breathe. Allowing in small, careful breaths, I rest my palm against the wall to keep me balanced.

Loud footsteps sound from behind my shoulder, until I'm pressed up against the wall of the dining room. Jaxon's eyes glare into mine, silently screaming at me, demanding an answer. Although, I have no answer. I've made a scene in front of his sisters and I am speechless as to what I could possibly say.

"What the fuck," he harshly whispers, shaking my shoulders as if to snap me out of it. "What was that?"

"You kissed me," I murmur.

"Oh, did I?" he humors me, enraged. His sharp jawline clenches shut, twitching.

"And, I didn't know how to respond."

"So, you run out of the room like a chicken with its head cut off?" He growls, releasing an exasperated breath. "Do you have any idea what you've just done?"

My eyes widen with innocence. "I don't know."

"Sasha," he groans, his grip on my shoulders tightening. I flinch from the pressure, and he immediately releases me. "What the fuck were you thinking? You can't just push me away and make a run for it when I kiss you in front of my sisters. You could have destroyed our arrangement. They could call us out on our fake engagement right now, if they really think everything through. I can't believe you had the nerve to do something so ignorant, so illogical—"

"You told me that we would never kiss again," I shakily state, welcoming anger. "And then you kissed me, Master—"

"Jesus," he groans, pressing his finger against my quivering lips, anxiously glancing around the room. "Jaxon. It's Jaxon, Sasha. What are you thinking? What is the matter with you?"

My heart thumps hard. "I don't know," I whisper.

"Come here." He takes my hand, practically dragging me into the bathroom with him as he closes the door. Our eyes meet, and it's more than obvious he's boiling with rage. "You've vomited. You have the stomach bug. It came on suddenly." He flushes the toilet, I'm assuming for sound effects.

"Yes, Mas—"

He glares at me, his eyes staring dangerously into mine.

"I'm sorry," I quietly say, dropping my gaze to my wobbling legs. "I feel like I'm going to pass out."

"Christ," he breathes, reaching me in a split second, holding me against him. "Calm down. This is absurd."

My head becomes light, and my vision is fuzzy. I'm suddenly seeing stars, gripping the front of his suit for dear life to keep myself upright.

Finally, my breathing starts to slow, and the small room around us ceases to spin. Without the slightest bit of warning, there's a knock upon the door.

"Jaxon?" Crystal asks from the other side.

"Yes, we're in here. Sasha got sick. We should be out soon," he explains, sounding smooth, and honest.

There's a gasp. "Oh, no," Blake sadly whines.

"That's awful. Take your time, guys," Crystal coos.

The sound of their footsteps walking away has us relieved, and we quickly step away from one another. Jaxon flushes the toilet once more. It was very fortunate that with his quick thinking, we have successfully gotten out of this predicament.

A few minutes pass by, and it seems to drag on for eternity. He won't even look at me. It's clear I've disappointed him, yet I couldn't care less. Pushing every thought into the back of my mind, we leave the restroom together and find his family gathered in the living room.

Lucy catches my gaze and sadly sighs. "I heard you've gotten sick, dear. Are you all right? Is there anything I can get you?" she nicely offers.

"We may have ginger ale," Blake suggests with a grin. "And saltines. They really help when you're not feeling well. Mom says they're the quickest cure to easing an upset stomach."

Crystal stares at me blankly, arms folded over her chest.

I nod. "Sure."

"Perhaps, she needs rest," Jaxon announces. "Sorry for our short stay."

"Don't be silly," Lucy tells him, pecking a quick kiss on his cheek. "We understand."

He nods once, forcing a grin.

"I hope you feel better soon, Sasha." Lucy gently places her hand on my shoulder. "Come back when you can."

"Lots of television and soup," Blake says with a giggle, hugging me briefly.

"Yes, definitely." I attempt to express a realistic smile, turning to Crystal. "It was really nice to meet you. I hope we can catch up soon."

"Lunch sometime, maybe?" she suggests. "I know some

really cute cafés downtown. I can show you around one of these days."

"That would be great. I'd really like that."

JAXON GETS CALLED into Edwards Enterprises in the late afternoon. Having the whole house to myself, I'm unsure what I could do to pass the time.

The California breeze is warm, inviting, and calling out to me. Throwing on my swimsuit, along with a light throw over, I decide to explore the beach behind his house.

The path that leaves from the back of the mansion is a short walk, my toes buried in the sand within minutes. The waves are slow, peaceful, filling me with tranquility as I watch them crash against the shore. The air is humid and the seagulls are screeching. It smells like seaweed and saltwater, the perfect combination. Breathing it in, and closing my eyes, I smile to myself.

Until, I'm reminded by everything that's happened to me in the past seventy-two hours.

My smile fades, and I head back to the house.

So much for exploring the beach.

It's not long before I realize that I've clearly pushed my limits earlier this morning when we were with his family. The fact of the matter is, I was shocked. I found myself enraged and confused as to how he could even consider kissing me after hurting me so badly. He made it clear that we were to never kiss again, and I was comfortable with that. The second his lips touched mine, I knew that I couldn't handle it, couldn't fake it.

I didn't want anything to do with his lips again.

Those soft, warm lips.

Shaking my head in aggravation, I sigh, hating how I had let my emotions get in the way. After thinking it through for a while, I decide that having dinner ready on the table for him might make up for my bad behavior.

Fortunately, I remember his favorite meal he had informed me of during the car ride to his parent's house the first time around. Hopefully, this will eliminate any punishments.

Two hours later, I've cleaned the house, and everything seems to sparkle. After taking a long, steaming shower, I prepare our dinner and find myself able to relax again. This is my job, after all.

Only minutes away from finishing cooking, I hear the front door clash open. Cleaning off my hands with a paper towel, I quickly make my way to the living room.

Jaxon lifts his head, taking in my appearance before looking away.

"I've cleaned the house." I grin, silence filling the space between us as he remains unimpressed. "I'm also cooking dinner."

He places his briefcase down onto the glass table, seeming drained.

"Your favorite," I quietly add in, dreading the eerie silence.

The aroma in the air is evident, I'm sure he's breathing it in with admiration, although he's completely unresponsive. All I feel is tension.

Suddenly, he meets my gaze. "Good," he presses, his voice firm as he looks over everything I've cleaned. He nods with approval. "And you've prepared my favorite meal?"

"Yes, Master," I reply.

His facial expression continues to remain hardened, on high alert. "Good."

"Well, is there anything you'd like for me to do, or should I get back to cooking?"

He shakes his head, breaking our eye contact. "I'm fine."

Turning on his heel, he begins to walk away, and I sigh in defeat.

"Thank you, Sasha."

And with that, he's gone, leaving me standing alone.

You're welcome, Jax.

The room is quiet as I set the dining room table for two, wondering if I should ask before I assume he'd like my company. Serving the heavenly scented food onto our plates, I hear him stepping through the doorway, catching a glimpse of him from the corner of my eye. Keeping my gaze locked on our plates, I head back to the counter to grab my glass of red wine. I don't deserve a beer.

Lifting my head, I spot him standing behind his chair, as handsome as a God. With his wet, disheveled hair and glistening arms, it's clear he's just gotten out of the shower.

Sitting down, he eyes me silently.

"What would you like to drink?" I ask, motionless.

Jaxon clears his throat, rubbing his lean fingers against his slight stubble. "A beer would be exquisite," he dryly responds.

Of course.

Placing the bottle in front of him, I sit across the table and sip my wine. He begins to cut through his steak, and I feel ridiculous as I watch him eat. Finally, it's clear. Satisfaction, cooked to perfection, exactly to his liking.

"How was your day?" I ask, regretting it the second he lifts his gaze.

He cocks his head to the side, chewing in silence.

I nervously swallow.

"My day? Well, besides my morning, everything went smoothly."

Dropping my gaze to my plate, I hold my breath. "How did your meeting go?"

"I get what I want."

When I look across the table, his eyes beam confidence, a crooked smirk playing at the corner of his lips.

Cocky bastard.

Several minutes pass, and he hasn't even touched his drink.

"Did I get you the wrong beer?" I wonder. "I can get you another."

I begin to stand, until he slams his hand on the table, and I flinch.

"Stop," he says, barely audible.

I stare at him with confusion.

He sharply exhales, leaning forward ever so slightly. "What are you doing?"

I blink, unsure of what he means, and how to respond.

"What is this? Hmm?" His eyes narrow, and his lips part.

"I'm doing what you've asked for," I simply answer, my fingertips pressing hard against the edge of the table. "Being a good little girl, pleasing my Dominant." This rolls off my tongue with nothing other than sarcasm. *Shit.* "Isn't that what you want from me?"

He sits up in his seat, folding his arms across his chest as his biceps flex. There's a stare-down between the two of us as we stay quiet, and I don't dare to speak first.

"Would you like to know what I truly want?" he asks, his voice throaty. "To have my fucking cock buried deep in your ass."

I gasp for air, and he pushes out his chair, standing tall.

"Playroom, now."

"What?"

"Get in my playroom, Sasha. I won't tell you again."

Swiftly rushing to my feet, I leave the dining and kitchen area at once, obeying his command. My heart is pounding. Everything becomes a blur until I'm standing in the middle of Mr. Edward's playroom, adrenaline once again kicking into my system.

"I'm being punished," I carefully state, turning to look in his direction. "Why?"

"Please, save yourself some dignity," he retorts, closing the door. Jaxon faces me, slowly approaching me until he's towering over my small frame. Somehow, I manage to hold his gaze, cursing at how powerful he is. "You know exactly what you're being punished for."

"But I've cleaned and cooked for you," I argue.

There's a low growl in his chest. "Do not move from this spot."

I stay silent, disobedient. I have no fear. I feel nothing.

"What was that?" he urges, stepping so close our bodies are nearly touching.

"Yes, Master."

He strides over to the dresser, retrieving a blindfold along with something I'm not familiar with. My imagination wanders. I'm frozen in place as he walks past me to another platform holding unique instruments. The moment he turns around, my heart nearly stops. There's an object which is in the shape of a bar, shackles attached on both sides.

Holy shit.

Very slightly, I make an involuntary movement, jerking my body toward the door.

"Go ahead. Do it." His voice is daring, and dark. I feel as if I'm a dangerous predator's prey in this very moment. "I'd enjoy the chase."

"I'm sorry, Master," I completely give in, lowering my head. "Punish me, please."

For a moment, there's no response. Although when our eyes lock, he seems to be shocked, completely taken back.

"You deserve it," he breathes.

He's right. I deserve to be punished for the way I behaved earlier today. I could have ruined everything for both of us. I deserve this.

Jaxon frowns. "Remove your clothes, Sasha."

"Yes, Master." Slowly, I strip off my clothes until I'm standing naked before him.

"Good girl," he purrs. "Now lean over the baseboard of the bed."

I do exactly as he says, when in one swift motion, he links something around my wrists, cuffing me to the post. Tugging slightly, the pressure cuts against my skin. He cuffs the other as well until I'm unable to move my arms, stretched out for him.

Exposed.

He presses the front of his body against my backside. "You were a naughty girl this morning, Sasha," he whispers against my ear. "Although you've tried to make up for your bad behavior by cleaning my house and cooking me dinner, I'm still unhappy with you. Do you have something to say to me?"

"I'm sorry, Master. That was wrong of me."

"It was."

"I'm sorry," I softly repeat.

He releases a small breath. "You're forgiven."

Turning to sneak a glimpse of him, he pulls his shirt over his head, exposing his masculine body. I can't help but feel the wetness pool between my thighs as I watch him feverishly, eagerly. Once he catches me staring, I quickly look away.

"You still need to be taught a lesson." His warm, bare chest presses against my back. "Are you ready to be fucked hard?"

"Yes, Master."

He spreads my legs apart with one fast movement of his foot. Looking down, I watch in suspense as he fastens the shackles of the long, metal bar around my ankles, ensuring my legs remain spread wide open for him. I can't be any more exposed than this.

As much as I hate to admit it to myself, I want him. I want to feel him inside me. I want him to destroy me in every possible way. My body is pleading for him, desperate for every inch of him.

His hands slowly trail up my legs, inner thighs, and stop once they reach my sex.

"Well," he groans. "It feels like someone wants to be punished."

"No," I quietly say. "That's not why I'm wet."

"Did that sound like a question to you, slave?"

That word.

The word slave once turned me off, and left me with an indescribable feeling of doubt and disgust. Once upon a time.

Now, it means nothing to me.

"No, it didn't. I'm sorry, Master."

"Have you ever been flogged before, Sasha?"

Shaking my head, my heart races at the thought. "No, Master."

"There's a first for everything." He lightly caresses my back, suddenly tying a ponytail around my hair, pulling it out of the way. "Bend over and stick that beautiful ass out for me."

My body tenses, and my endorphins already begin to flow at the thought of what he's going to do to me. My breathing becomes shallow.

My thighs are wet, and I am pleading to be fucked into oblivion. Suddenly, the light disappears, cutting out entirely as he secures the blindfold over my eyes.

Without hesitation, I obey, leaning forward.

"Good girl."

CHAPTER 18

My heart rate quickens, skipping several beats, thumping so wildly it's as if I've just run a marathon. My conscience diminishes, and anxiety sets in. The lack of motion in my body leaves me as still as a stone.

Yet, I'm trembling at the same time, desperate to know what is coming next. Paranoia creeps up on me. A dull ringing sounds in my ears, as I concentrate on the sound of my heart.

Drumming loudly, pounding.

"Do you remember your safe word, Sasha?"

His voice is powerful, bursting through the room.

"Yes," I quietly reply. "It's black, Master."

"Do not hesitate to use it if you feel it's needed."

"Yes, Master."

Gently, he brushes the side of my arm, his touch sending goosebumps over what feels like every inch of my body.

"I will walk you through this," he firmly announces, resting his hand against my upper back. "We will start off light. Am I clear?"

"Yes, Master."

The first snap of the whip against my shoulder blade

makes me flinch, and it stings against my flesh. Although, just as suddenly as it appeared, it fades away. My pulse begins to slow, and I come to realize that he is not planning on torture.

Gasping for air, I try to ease my built-up nerves, disappointment taking over. It strikes me as terrifying to think that I was so desperate to feel something, that I would really settle for pain.

At this very moment, I understand how corrupted I've become.

"There is one, slave," he purrs. "Now tell me, how many do you think you deserve? Three, five, ten, twenty?"

Rhetorical questions. He's already made up his mind.

Whish.

The second time is far worse, a moan escaping my trembling lips. This time the flogger strikes my behind, and feels very different than his hand. It's a foreign feeling, rough against my skin, unlike his smooth palm.

"There will be ten," Mr. Edwards breathes beside my ear. The heady scent of his cologne has me enticed. "The number is nice and round, just like your ass."

Whish.

My arms and back tense up, and my skin burns. Until unexpectedly, my muscles start to relax, and I'm left with beautiful sensations like no other. The light strikes continue, slowly, torturously.

Whish.

My bottom feels as if it's on fire, yet pleasure consumes every fiber of my being. It's a delicious attack, and I feel ecstatic as it seems to relieve every ounce of my stress.

The pain goes straight to my pleasure centers, my inner thighs are drenched, my nipples are puckered, and my stomach is quivering. There's something so sensual about this scene, so intimate.

Whish.

"Yes," I moan. My arms become light as I pull hard on the cuffs. "Please."

"Yes?" he asks, his voice low, content.

"More, please," I somehow manage to speak through my dry throat. "Please, Master."

He slightly groans, seeming satisfied. Appalled. "As you wish."

Jaxon Edwards continues his gentle strokes of the flogger, traveling from my buttocks, back to my shoulder blades. Caressing me with the leather, easing up, before coming down with more force.

My breaths are uneven, and I'm moaning loudly, giving in tremendously to the incredible sensations. I'm in a state of ecstasy as he works his magic upon my skin.

"Oh, Sasha." He sharply exhales, gently rubbing the stinging skin of my behind, attempting to ease the sting. "Having you so eager for more has made me more eager to give it to you."

Whish.

I tense up, crying out to him.

"Fuck," he growls, wrapping his arms around me, breathing in my hair. "You are something else, Sasha."

Gasping for air, I begin to come down from my high.

"What do you want?"

Once again, my body betrays my mind. "You," I reply with certainty.

With that, he presses the tip of his cock against my slick entrance. Unable to move my legs due to the restraint, I push back against him. He pulls away, breaking our skin to skin contact. I cry out in desperation, needing to have him.

To *feel* him.

"Now, now, slave." He runs his fingers through my hair, tugging tight on the strands.

Suddenly, he enters me. Moaning with urgency, he fills me

completely. Buried inside my tightness. My walls clench hard around him, holding him hostage. He pushes into me over and over, and pleasure ignites within me; mind, body, and soul. Writhing against his waist, my climax is already building.

Thrust after thrust, he hammers into me. With each grunt and sharp breath, there's the loud sound of our skin smacking. It only seems to make me feel more. He's merciless, forceful, fucking me straight into oblivion just like I had asked for.

My orgasm approaches steadily as his movements become stronger, deeper, his fingertips digging into my hips.

Finding myself unable to control myself, I'm on the brink of the edge. Without any warning, he removes himself.

Disappointment floods through me as I hear his final groans, taunting me as he finds his release. I'm left with nothing, other than pure sexual frustration, my orgasm pleading to be fulfilled.

Although, this was exactly his intention.

This was my punishment.

"Tell me what you're feeling, Sasha," Jaxon commands, removing my blindfold.

Staring frantically into his eyes, I become numb. "Disappointment," I softly say. "Frustration."

"Well, I'm glad you now understand how I felt this morning." He smugly grins, only for a moment, trying his best to get a reaction out of me. I'm left glaring at him, an inconceivable feeling of anger beaming through me.

Finally, instead of screaming at him, I decide to lower my head.

Submissively.

"I'm sorry, Master."

His eyes turn cold, shielded. It's clear he was not expecting this response. My heart drops into the pit of my stomach the moment he blindfolds me once more.

There're soft footsteps, and then the sound of the door slamming.

I feel empty, as my wrists are cuffed to the frame of the bed, my ankles are shackled to the restraint, and the blindfold covers my eyes.

A part of me wonders how long he's going to leave me here, how long he's going to be gone. Would he leave me here for an hour? Would he leave me here until morning? Would Mr. Edwards do something like that to me?

Yes, he would, because I'm his slave.

That's all I'll ever be to him.

Time slowly passes, and finally, the door opens. It's only seconds before I feel him unfastening the straps around my ankles, and then he undoes the cuffs around my wrists. He removes the blindfold, and turns me around to face him.

Our stare is complicated, intense.

"Would you prefer for me to stop using the word slave?" he asks, the tension in the room becoming much lighter. I blink up at him, startled by his question. "You had been so against it when we first had met, yet now, you don't even bat an eye."

"I don't mind it."

His jaw twitches, and his shoulders tense. "Why?"

"Because that's all I am to you. Your slave."

"Sasha," he says, his face softening. He steps forward, hesitating before he lightly brushes his fingertips against my cheek. "What's happening to you?"

He shakes his head, and turns his back to me.

"Did I do something?" I ask. "Did I say something wrong?"

"Go take a shower while I finish eating."

Once again, he's uninviting, guarded. Without wasting another second, I do exactly as I'm told, leaving the playroom in silence.

THE WATER FEELS incredible as it trails down my skin, easing every sore muscle. After I've spent far too long enjoying the warmth, I dress into a silky white nightgown, and find myself wanting to sleep. What I had experienced in his playroom has left me drained, ready to take in the feeling of the blankets wrapped tightly around my body.

As I make my way down the long, spiraling staircase, I can't seem to find Jaxon anywhere. Although, the sliding glass door is wide open.

Stepping through the doorway and out into the darkness, Jaxon appears to be staring up at the sky full of stars.

"Excuse me," I speak up, as he turns to acknowledge my presence.

"Yes?" His tone is monotone, flat.

"I was wondering if you need me for anything, Master," I say, my voice trailing off. "Or if I can go to sleep now—"

"—Jaxon."

The moonlight makes his skin shimmer, and his eyes gleam. Suddenly, I realize what he has just said, drawing a blank.

"What?" I murmur.

"Jaxon. It's Jaxon," he corrects me, running his hand through his hair. "No, you know what, address me as whatever you'd like. I truly don't care."

Trying to process what he's just said, I shrug my shoulders. "Master just feels easy, more comfortable."

"More comfortable?" he snarls, striding toward me. "What are you talking about? Calling me Master makes you feel more comfortable now?"

"Yes."

"Where is this coming from?" Jaxon is demanding, on edge, his face mere inches from mine. His eyes are beaming, enraged, catching me off guard.

I frown. "I'm giving you honesty."

"No, what you're giving me is complete shit!" He snaps,

and I flinch. Staring up at him helplessly, I remain silent. "You know what, fine. Master is fine. Call me whatever you want. Do whatever you want. Actually, just go to bed. That is what you want from me, right? My permission to fucking sleep?"

"Yes."

He searches my eyes with his, gazing at me compassionately, yet with disgust at the same time. Pressing his lips into a firm, straight line, he swiftly turns on his heel, and heads further into the darkness.

"What do you want from me?" My voice comes out unsteady, confused.

Halting himself to an abrupt stop, all I can hear is the sound of the crickets, the gentle wind, and my uneven breaths. Time has stopped. I can't feel anything, other than my pounding heart thumping wildly against my ribcage.

Eventually, he turns to face me, looking straight into my eyes. "I don't know," he whispers.

"Goodnight," I say.

He remains motionless, silent. With that, I leave his sight.

THE BLANKETS KEEP me warm as I snuggle into them. The room is dark, although the moon from the window creates a natural night light. My mind is finally able to shut down.

Until out of nowhere, there's a gentle knock upon my door.

My eyes shoot open and I grow curious, keeping still. There's another small knock shortly after as I rush out of bed, realizing I was not imagining it. Flipping on the light switch, I pull open the door, shocked to see Jaxon standing in the hallway.

His gaze remains locked on an object in his grasp, and it's almost impossible to figure out what it is from the way he's moving it around in his palm. Without prolonging this moment any further, his eyes meet mine, and he holds out his hand.

"This is for you," he breathes, searching every inch of my face. "We need to ensure that our fake engagement is as realistic as possible. I tried my very best to pick out something I thought you'd prefer." He briefly hesitates. "I hope you like it."

Looking away from his troubled face, he carefully places a small, velvet box onto the center of my palm. A dramatic gasp escapes me, as I stare up at him once more in disbelief.

"Goodnight, Sasha."

Staring at his backside as he walks away, I am left speechless. Standing quietly in my doorway, I struggle hard to catch my breath.

Closing my door and sitting down on the bed, I brace myself, trying to contain my racing thoughts. The moment I lift the lid, my heart nearly stops. It's the most beautiful ring I've ever seen.

CHAPTER 19

*I*ts elegance and simplicity is far beyond my wildest dreams. With a platinum band, outlined in several small emeralds, the main diamond leaves my hands trembling.

It's much larger than I had anticipated, shimmering brightly as the light makes contact. I am fascinated.

Reaching in ever so slowly, I remove the beautiful ring from the placement of the small, velvet box. How could he surprise me with something so gorgeous?

This was beyond thoughtful of him, especially in a time where I didn't think he could be thoughtful.

What does this man want from me?

Carefully pushing it back into the slit in the box, I close the lid. Placing it into the top drawer of my nightstand, I turn off the light and crawl back into bed.

Wrapping myself back into the silk sheets, I finally fall asleep.

Boom.

Awaking from my deep slumber, jolting up, I'm now on alert. Something has happened. Glancing over to the clock, I read that it's a little past two o'clock in the morning. Has someone broken into the house? Surely, with his security systems, this most likely isn't the case. Although, curiosity does get the best of me.

Peaking my head outside of my bedroom door, silence overwhelms me. Maybe I have dreamt it?

Making my way downstairs, footsteps from the living room grasp my attention. My gaze sets on Jaxon, casually standing beside the fireplace that's been lit.

Suddenly, our eyes lock.

"Well, well, well. Look who it is."

His playful, yet sarcastic tone, sends a wave of confusion over me. The moment he stumbles to the side, I understand what's going on.

"Little slave girl." Jaxon chuckles. "I like that name, don't you? It has a nice ring to it."

"You're drunk," I observe.

He retrieves a glass of whiskey from the table, throwing it back in one sip.

"Drunk? Me, intoxicated?" He scowls, motioning to himself with his thumb, before smirking. "Okay, okay. Fuck. You caught me."

"What was that sound?" Glancing around the room, I'm unable to spot anything out of the ordinary. "It was really loud."

"That sound was rage," he bleakly replies. "I got angry."

"About what?"

He frowns, shooting an irritated stare my way. "You care?" he dramatically gasps, stumbling on his feet for a moment. "I am shocked. Truly, I am."

"Did you break something?" I ask, stepping closer.

"What happened to addressing me as Master?" he asks, his

voice booming, eyebrows knitted together. "Master this, Master that. Can I brush my teeth, Master, or brush my hair? Can I go to sleep now, Master?" He huffs, pouring himself another glass of whiskey, and spilling some onto the table in the process.

"I don't think that's a good idea," I anxiously blurt out.

He holds the glass in his hand, waving it around in the air. "You actually asked me for permission to fucking sleep. Ha! Unbelievable."

"There's no need to be mean."

Placing the glass down, he stumbles to the side, before catching my nervous gaze. I have never seen him this way before. It almost strikes me as odd. Suddenly, he walks toward me.

He stops mere inches away, his eyes staring vulnerably into mine. "I'm acting like an asshole, aren't I?" He mumbles, slurring his words.

"I think it's time for bed," I suggest.

"Time for bed," he mocks me, rolling his eyes. "You're bossy tonight. I don't like it."

"I'm only trying to help."

"There's no need for that, baby."

I sigh, completely aggravated with his dull humor. "What did you break, Master?"

"Ah, fuck," he snarls, running his hand through his hair. "There it is again."

Walking around him, it doesn't take me long before I spot the bookshelf lying flat behind the couch, books spattered everywhere. My breathing hitches, and I wonder if I should begin cleaning this mess now, or if it can wait until the morning.

"Leave it," he commands, as I turn to look at him from across the room. "I'll do it."

"It's my job."

"And I'm telling you, that I will do it," he loudly slurs. "It's my mess, Sasha. Allow me to fix it."

Gazing at one another silently, I wonder if he's really talking about the bookshelf, or something else entirely.

What has gotten into him?

Jaxon frowns. "Why did you come down here?"

"I was sleeping, and the sound of the bookshelf falling was so loud it woke me. I came down here to see what it was because I was worried about—" I hesitate, taking in a deep breath.

"About what?" he urges.

"I was worried that maybe someone broke in. That there was an intruder."

"They wouldn't dare," he presses, pulling me against his body.

"What are you doing?" I ask, startled as he holds me closer.

"You're lying. Tell me that you care. Tell me that you still care," he drunkenly pleads, his hypnotizing, blue eyes widening, desperately searching mine. "Do it! Tell me that you care. Right this instant."

"Tell you that I care about what?" I dare to ask.

His face hardens, and our eye contact immediately breaks. "Fuck this," he groans, releasing me at once, reaching for his glass before tossing it into the fireplace.

The flames erupt from the leftover liquor, sizzling, glass shattering against the logs of wood.

I blink up at him, horrified. "Are you okay?"

"Just peachy."

"Let me help you to your room," I offer.

"I'm a grown man, Sasha. I'll be fine," he breathes, hurrying past me. "Just go back to bed."

Unexpectedly, he stumbles to the side, and just in time I happen to grasp his arm. Draping it over my shoulders, I link my arms around his waist and try my best to keep him upright, even though he's far too heavy for my small body to handle.

He looks down into my eyes and shakes his head. "I said I'm fine," he murmurs, pulling away, until he stumbles again.

We crash against the wall. "Just let me help you," I breathe out, holding him tighter. Hating this. "Please."

"Fine."

Stunned with this whole situation, I help him as we make our way out of the living room. Walking with him pressed against me, we slowly stumble down the hallway.

The door pushes open, and I'm in awe as we step into his bedroom. It's so plain, with furniture only. His bed is huge, almost bigger than a king-size. The ceiling is high, and his main window is large. I get the sense of loneliness in here, a longing for more.

It smells like *him*. Breathing it in, we finally make it to his bed.

Lifting his arm from my shoulder, I help him ease his way onto the mattress, until he's resting motionless on his back. In one fast motion, he pulls off his shirt.

"Christ," he snarls, rubbing his closed eyes with his fists. "I can already feel a migraine approaching."

"I'll bring you Advil in the morning," I softly assure him.

"Beautiful," he mumbles, deeply sighing before gazing over at me. "Coffee and breakfast will be ready as well?"

"Of course."

"Exquisite."

"Goodnight, Master."

Turning away, I begin to leave, until he grasps my wrist. Forced to an abrupt stop, our gazes meet, and his dissatisfaction is evident. His eyes bore into mine, and he remains silent, making me feel as if I'm floating on cloud nine. The way he's looking at me is new, different.

"Wh—where are you going?" he nearly whispers.

"To my room."

He shakes his head.

"I don't understand," I say.

"Come here," he says, tugging on my wrist.

"I'm right here."

"No, closer," he presses, his jaw tightening when I don't move an inch. "I want you closer. I'm becoming quite impatient."

"I don't understand what you mean. I'm as close as I can get."

"I want you to lay next to me, Sasha," he says, his voice low, eager. "I want you to stay here. Stay until I'm asleep. Then you can go to your room. I, I just want you here with me right now."

Without questioning or disobeying, I sheepishly nod. "Okay."

He's so intoxicated, I doubt he will even remember any of this tomorrow. Walking around the other side of the bed, I crawl onto the mattress, sinking into the spot beside him. Taking in deep breaths, it's not long before he pulls me closer.

Momentarily looking at his face, his eyes are now shut and he appears to be relaxed. Without any warning, his fingertips stroke against the inside of my wrist, gently stroking my palm.

Suddenly, he pushes his fingers through mine.

Rolling onto his side to face me, he wraps his other arm around me. His bare chest radiates warmth. Running his fingers through my hair, he tries to comfort me in a way I wouldn't expect him to.

"I love you," Jaxon whispers.

My whole world stops.

My heart rate quickens, and my head becomes light. It's almost impossible to breathe. Jaxon Edwards has just confessed his love to me. How can this be?

". . .Marnie."

Within the blink of an eye, everything drastically changes.

Time stops as it registers in my brain, and I come crashing back to reality. So many thoughts seem to take over my mind, yet all I can focus on is the fact that he has just called me another woman's name.

CHAPTER 20

*H*e's drunk, far beyond words can possibly describe. The truth is, because of this, I don't know whether I can take anything he says seriously. Perhaps I'm dreaming, or perhaps, I'm not. Drunken words are sober thoughts, supposedly.

Marnie.

Her name echoes in my mind. Does this woman really exist? Who is she? Where is she? Why hasn't he spoken of her until now? Millions of questions haunt me until I feel blue in the face.

Staring over at Jaxon, I don't dare to look away. His eyes remain closed and he seems to be so peaceful, so utterly innocent. My insides are boiling with rage. His chest rises, up and down with each breath, and my heart pounds vigilantly.

Minutes must pass by, and I'm shocked at how calm I've become. I should be waking him up, shaking him hard, demanding for him to explain himself.

Although, I am numb.

Suddenly, he turns his head to the side, and rolls onto his

back. He releases a small breath, fast asleep. What made him this way? Did Marnie make him this way? I must find out.

"Jaxon?"

He remains quiet, not even the slightest stir.

I can't do this.

Pushing every thought to the back of my head, I unlock our hands, and move my legs over the side of the bed. After making my way across his room, I stand still in the center of his doorway. Turning to give him one last look, I find myself uneasy, confused.

When I enter the living room, the flames of the fire have become dim. He must have been very drunk to have started a fire in this season. Cleaning the whiskey off the table with a dishcloth, I then make my way over to the bookcase to examine the aftermath.

Kneeling, I begin to collect the novels. Gathering most of them together into a neat pile, anger consumes me again.

Tossing a book at the wall, I hug my knees to my chest.

Breathe, Sasha.

My once bland life has now turned into a series of unthinkable events. As much as I resent him for what he has done to me, a part of me still can't help but care for him.

That's the worst part of all.

Leaving the tipped over bookshelf and opened novels on the floor, I quickly make my way to my room. Crawling back into bed, I tightly shut my eyes, praying for the darkness to swallow me whole.

THE SUNNY DAY has rays of light pouring into the kitchen, brightening the beautiful space around me as I turn on a pot of coffee. After searching through the cabinets, I eventually find a bottle of Advil. It's a little after ten o'clock, and I'm exhausted after hardly getting any sleep all night.

Yawning, I retrieve a glass of water for Jaxon.

Slowly opening his door, darkness welcomes me. His curtains are thick, removing any source of daylight from the outside. Making out his figure in the center of the king-size bed, it's evident that he's still fast asleep. Lying flat on his stomach, he's sprawled out over the sheets, and his muscular back is exposed.

"Morning."

There's silence.

"Master," I hesitate, correcting myself. "Jaxon?"

"Mmm," he groans, replying so abruptly that I flinch. "What?"

"Good morning."

"Is it?"

"You wanted me to wake you. It's after ten—"

"I'm not moving," he blatantly objects.

A minute must pass by, as I continue to become more aggravated, waiting patiently for him to make another movement. Although, there's nothing. Placing the pills and glass onto his nightstand, I pull open his curtains, and the sun's bright rays invade the room.

The moment the light reaches his face, he cringes. "Fuck."

"I have Advil for your headache."

"What headache?" He sharply exhales, sitting upright as the light beams straight into his eyes. Immediately, he holds up his hand, attempting to block it out as he sits on the edge of the bed. He pushes his face into his palms. "Ah, this headache."

"Here," I offer, holding out the glass and pills between us.

Dropping his hands, he looks up at me, eyes squinted. Jaxon accepts the pills and pops them into his mouth, and chugs down every sip of water. Lowering his gaze to the floor, he pinches the bridge of his nose between his fingers.

"What the hell happened?"

"What happened?" I ask.

He doesn't remember.

"Yes, Sasha," he breathes, sighing as his eyes meet mine. "What happened?"

"A lot."

"Tell me," he demands, placing the glass back onto the nightstand. "Everything."

"You woke me up in the middle of the night by knocking over the bookshelf in the living room. You were really drunk. You mocked me and tossed a glass into the fireplace. You could barely walk to your room on your own without falling over, so I helped you. I put you to bed and—" I pause, unsure about whether I should mention the most important part.

His ocean blue eyes pour into mine. "And, what?"

My lips part, but I can't speak.

"Dammit, Sasha—"

"—And you called me another woman's name."

His eyes widen. "I did what?"

"You called me another woman's name," I softly repeat, and he stands. "Marnie."

"Marnie?" he questions, the name sounding so strange and foreign coming from his mouth.

I nod.

"You must have heard me wrong."

"I know what I heard," I press. "You called me Marnie."

He steps closer. "I don't know anyone by that name."

Liar.

"Honesty goes for the both of us, right?" I challenge him.

"Yes." He stands. "Why did you do it?"

"Do what?"

"Take care of me. Why did you take care of me last night?"

"You needed me," I answer, and he flinches. There's a

pained new expression that claims his face. "So, I was there for you."

He turns away. "Coffee," he mutters. "I need to make coffee."

"I've already made a pot, *Jaxon*."

Facing me quickly, he crookedly grins. There's a sparkle in his eyes. "There it is. I've missed that."

I stay quiet.

"Well, then."

He gestures to the door with his hand.

Once we step into the kitchen, the heavenly aroma of freshly perked coffee fills the air, sending my senses into overload. As I grasp the handle of the pot, he keeps me still by cupping his hand lightly over mine. His chest brushes against my back, and I shudder at the warmth.

"That's not necessary," he quietly says. "I can take it from here. Thank you, Sasha."

"You're welcome."

I step to the side, and he retrieves two mugs from the cabinet and fills them. "You've also cooked breakfast?"

"I have."

Looking my way, he frowns. "It's not deserved on my part, is it?"

I stay quiet.

"Thank you, Sasha."

Sitting down at the table together, neither of us dare to speak a single word, when suddenly, it hits me.

Jolting in my seat, all the color drains from my face. Jaxon has made it clear that he has never met a woman with the name of Marnie, and that leaves one unsolved mystery.

There's still one unanswered question.

"That wasn't all," I rush out. "You said something else."

He lifts his head from his plate, his attention now focused on me. "Last night?"

"Yes."

"What else?"

"I love you," I reply, and he becomes still. "You said I love you."

Leaning back in his chair, he acts as if he hasn't heard me.

"You said I love you, as bright as day. If I misunderstood you, and you've never met a woman named Marnie, then that means you were talking to me."

Pressing his mouth into a firm, straight line, our eyes lock once more. There's passion built up within them, creating such a heated moment that I've suddenly become breathless. We've both become paralyzed to the point where we are unable to speak, to move, to even blink. This is important to me. I need this moment.

I need to know.

"Did you mean it?"

"I blacked out," he carefully answers. "No, Sasha. I didn't."

A sharp breath escapes from me, and I immediately look away from his guarded eyes. "Good."

"How I acted last night, what I did, that was wrong of me. Allow me to make it up to you. Today is an extremely busy day for me. I have meetings back to back. They're crucial, or else I would reschedule."

"You don't need to make it up to me. It's fine."

"No," he states, leaning forward. "It isn't fine. Pick out something nice to wear for later."

"For what?"

"I'm taking you out to dinner tonight, Ms. Pierce."

With that, he pushes out his chair, and dismisses himself from the table.

THE CLOCK STRIKES EIGHT O'CLOCK. I'm ready just in time,

staring at my reflection in the mirror. My black dress ends a few inches above my knees, the elegant gold patterns matching my heels to perfection. My hair has bouncy curls, my makeup is beautifully done. I can hardly recognize myself.

Once I reach the top of the staircase, Jaxon appears at the bottom, and this is the first time I've seen him since this morning. My nerves kick in, and a blush settles on my cheeks.

"Sasha," he murmurs, gazing over every inch of me as I arrive at the last step. "You're so beautiful."

Taking in the sight of him, I'm left speechless. It's baffling to realize the effect this man still manages to have on me. He's wearing a black, tailored suit with a white-collar shirt beneath, along with a plain, black tie. His dark hair is brushed neatly, and he's clean shaved.

And those eyes.

Those beautiful, blue eyes.

He remains silent, his expression masked, and from the way he's staring down at me it leaves my stomach in a knot.

"Shall we?" he asks.

Placing my hand lightly in his, he plants a kiss against my skin.

I weakly grin. "We shall."

CHAPTER 21

There's a black hummer limo parked idle in the driveway. As I find my seat, the interior has me entranced, drawn to every detail.

There're neon lights at the floor's surface and above us, shining vivaciously through the ceiling. With the black leather seats, and bottles of champagne resting alongside one of the rows, this feels like a fantasy come to life.

Gazing out the tinted windows, I watch our surroundings outside change as we glide down the highway. The lights downtown enhance the palm trees swaying slightly in the wind. It's a beautiful sight.

"Would you like a glass of champagne?" Jaxon asks, breaking the comfortable silence between us.

"Please," I reply.

He swiftly retrieves the bottle, and pours two glasses. My taste buds welcome the sweet and bubbly taste as I take the first sip.

"Where are we going?" I ask.

"One of the finest dining establishments around."

Twenty minutes must pass, until finally, we appear to be in

a wealthy area downtown. The trees, pillars, and light poles are strung up with white lights, glowing in the moonlight.

As we come to a stop at the curb of the restaurant, it's evident he wasn't lying about the fine dining.

"We've arrived," Jaxon announces, exiting the limo.

Placing my hand in his, I step out into the night, and the brisk air welcomes me.

We walk up the front steps hand in hand, striding toward the large front doors, before two doormen open them for us.

"Gentlemen," Jaxon says, nodding formally in their direction. "Appreciate it."

They lower their heads in unison.

It reminds me of the first night we had met, when the valet at the hotel couldn't seem to stop bowing in Jaxon's presence. Sighing quietly under my breath, we enter the elegant restaurant, greeted by dim lights and quiet chatter among the guests.

Jaxon sneaks his arm around my waist as we approach the host stand.

"Reservation for Edwards," he states, his tone booming masculinity. Power.

"Jaxon Edwards," the hostess says, a strong blush crossing her cheeks. "Yes, I see. Reservations for two. The special."

Her gaze meets mine, and for a split second, I'm able to see the envy behind her eyes. She gathers two menus and exchanges a silent stare with another hostess.

"Right this way," she announces, and we follow behind her.

There's a countless amount of people in the dining area, and an unimaginable number of servers weaving through tables.

Finally, the hostess brings us to a door, and she slowly slides it open. Jaxon has set up a private room for the two of us to ensure our complete privacy from the outside world.

This must have cost him an absolute fortune. My head

spins the moment I take in the seductive feel, the soft music, and beautifully decorated table in the center.

She leads us further into the room, and places our menus onto the table. Before I can even blink, Jaxon pulls out my chair like the perfect gentleman, waiting patiently. The weight on my shoulders builds up and I suddenly feel so much pressure. I never would have imagined him arranging something like this for me.

Not in a million years.

He sits across from me, not daring to take his eyes off mine for even a second. Jaxon Edwards has drastically changed. There's something off about him tonight, something different.

I just can't seem to put my finger on it.

Our hostess flirtatiously smiles in his direction, attempting to gain his attention. "Can I get you anything, Sir?"

"No," he smugly responds, his eyes deeply searching mine. "I have everything I need right in front of me."

MY STOMACH IS FULL, satisfied from the wonderful meal I have just mauled down in a matter of minutes. My mind is finally content. Listening to the soothing music, and sipping my expensive red wine, I'm more than relaxed.

When suddenly, Jaxon breaks the silence.

"Interesting."

"What?" I murmur, frozen.

"You've hardly said a word for the last hour," he observes. "You appear bored. You're not having any fun, are you?"

"I guess not," I boldly reply, his eyes slightly narrowing in response. "It was very thoughtful of you to bring me here, but no. Fun wouldn't be the right word to describe what I'm feeling."

He smirks. "Ouch."

"I'm just giving you honesty, Master."

"Sasha," he sharply breathes, glaring menacingly at me from across the table. "What did I say about addressing me as that outside the playroom? Would you like a hard spanking over my knee right now? Is that what this is?"

"It's a force of habit," I counter. "Forgive me?"

"You don't believe me, Sasha?" he asks. "I will pull up that little black dress, toss you onto this table, and spank your ass so hard and raw you won't be able to sit for days."

Gulping, I say nothing.

And he grins, humorously. "You are beyond difficult, Sasha."

"I'm sorry."

"For what?"

My lips part, yet I'm speechless.

Jaxon shakes his head in frustration. "You're like a broken record, constantly apologizing for anything and everything. Why don't you do us both a favor, and cut the shit."

I frown, confused. "I have no idea what you're talking about."

"You do," he firmly argues. "Stop this little charade of acting like you're a goddamn robot. I'm getting sick and tired of you telling me exactly what I want to hear. This isn't who you are, how you are."

He becomes quiet, and his face softens.

I am intrigued, curious. "How am I?"

"You're feisty. Determined. You never listen. You're always fighting me. It's like a goddamn ritual between us. If I say turn right, you turn left. If I say don't move, you run. But now," he hesitates, disturbed, and his face drops.

"Now, what?" I urge.

"You're *this*. I don't even know what *this* is."

"And?"

"And it's fucking hell."

"You're giving me mixed signals," I unthinkingly blurt out, completely fed up.

He grimaces.

"Everything was going great between us, especially at the cabin. We jumped in the lake, and had dinner under the stars. You told me a few funny stories about your childhood, and I told you my story, about my parents. Then, out of nowhere, you turned on me."

I stare at him, disgusted, shooting him daggers with my eyes.

He lowers his head. "I know."

"You told me that you want me to be your Submissive, only your Submissive. You told me you wanted me to obey you, to give in, and that's exactly what I've done. And, in the end, I'll go back home with one-hundred thousand dollars."

I silence myself.

Once he's noticed my hesitation, he nods. "Say it."

"If it wasn't for the money at the end of this, I'd already be gone."

Conflicted, and guarded, he leans back in his chair. I'm sure I've struck a nerve from the look in his eyes.

"You hate me. Don't you?"

His question comes out quiet, gentle. It leaves me more than confused, watching such a dominant man become so defeated, so concerned, when I didn't even believe he was capable of emotions.

"A part of me does," I softly admit. "And, another part of me doesn't. Can you blame me?"

He leans forward, resting his arms on the table. "I was wrong for going about it the way that I did. I was wrong, Sasha."

"Liar," I dryly mutter.

"I'm not lying."

"As if your words mean anything to me."

His expression becomes masked, completely unreadable. From the way he's staring at me from across the table, it leaves me uneasy. It's impossible to tell what he's thinking. I don't have the slightest idea on what to expect next.

"That. That is what I miss. The old you," Jaxon says. "I thought I wanted you to be my perfect Submissive. I honestly did. I've realized now, that's not what I want. You've changed so much, too much, and I'm responsible for it. I don't want you to feel this way anymore."

Holding my head high, I can't help becoming defensive.

"I'm fine the way I am," I press, concentrating on the flickering candle between us. "I feel better than I have in years."

"Now look who's lying."

"You know so much about me, don't you, Jaxon?" I retort, sarcasm thick in my tone. "Yet, I still know so little about you."

"Five minutes."

Flashing him an eager stare, my breathing quickens. "What?"

"You have five minutes to ask me anything."

My heart begins to hammer at the thought. "Anything?"

"Yes." Jaxon observes his Rolex, taking note of the time, before our eyes lock. "Anything."

"Right now?"

"Starting, now."

A rush of adrenaline consumes me at full force, and I know now that I'm going to take advantage of this opportunity.

"Why did you turn on me the morning at the cabin?" I ask.

"Pass."

"You said anything."

"I woke up and you were in my arms," he sincerely replies. "You looked beautiful, more beautiful than anyone or anything I'd seen in my entire fucking life. You were in my room, in my bed, with me. I was terrified I had allowed that to happen."

My heart pounds at the memory.

"That's why you turned on me?"

He nods once.

Pushing all emotions away, I remember the countdown.

"How did you get into the BDSM lifestyle?"

He stirs in his chair, uncomfortable. "A friend introduced me to it."

"Male or female?"

He releases a sharp breath. "A man, Sasha."

"Tell me more."

"He brought me along to a fetish club one night. A woman approached me while I was there, and she happened to be into the lifestyle already, living as a Submissive. I tried it out, and shortly after, we signed a contract."

I nod. "What was her name?"

"That's confidential."

"Have you ever had feelings for any of your previous Subs?"

"No," he strongly states. "I have not."

"Okay," I say, hesitating, pondering my next question. I must make this count. "What is the worst pain you've given to someone?"

His face hardens, and his shoulders visibly tense.

Seconds pass, and he remains quiet.

"Jaxon?"

"It was from flogging," he breathes. "So intensely, she was left with swollen welts across every inch of her back."

My heart pounds rapidly. My chest tightens. My face has become pale. I am stunned with his honesty, yet frightened at the same time. I shouldn't have asked. He's much darker than I could have imagined.

"That's awful," I nearly whisper. "That's inhumane."

"I'm a sadist, Sasha." His eyes sparkle. "Always have been, always will be."

"Did she report you?"

"No," he snarls, irritated. "Why on earth would she report me?"

"Because you hurt her."

"She was big on masochism, enjoyed high levels of pain. She asked me to do it, so I did."

"What if I wanted you to slit my wrists?" I question, testing him. "Would you do what I wanted, then?"

"Of course not," he groans, standing abruptly, facing his back toward me. I've crossed a line. "I would never cut your wrists. I would never hurt you. Never."

"Have you ever been in love?"

Immediately, he turns to me, and his eyes set on mine.

My heart sinks from the intimacy of this moment.

"Time is up," he quietly responds. "I'm not a good man, Sasha. I'm not going to act as if I'm not aware of this. It's complicated. I wish I could make you understand why I am the way I am, but I can't."

"We all have a dark side, Jaxon."

"My life is dark. There's never been any light. Until, *you*."

I stare up at him, blown away.

"Ever since the moment you appeared into my life, everything's changed. I was drawn to you because of how different you were. Most women have thrown themselves at me, yet you walked away from my car so easily. You didn't take my shit. You challenged me, and it made me so fucking mad."

"I'm sorry—"

Suddenly, he kneels by my side.

"Stop apologizing," he pleads, desperately searching my eyes. "I can't take it anymore. I will man up right now and tell you that I am so sorry, Sasha. I'm so fucking sorry for turning on you at the cabin after you poured your heart out to me. I'm so sorry I hurt you. This isn't what I wanted. I thought it was, but it's not. Please, Sasha."

Looking in his eyes, I can't help feeling numb, empty. Even after listening to everything he's just said, I feel absolutely nothing.

"I can't."

He swiftly takes my face between his hands, and everything around us becomes a blur. All I can see is him.

His eyes.

Those deep, intricate eyes.

"I'll get you back," he calmly says, staring straight into my soul. "I'll do everything in my power. That, I can assure you."

My breathing begins to pick up, and I squirm in my seat, locking my fingers around his wrists.

"I need to use the ladies room," I rush out, my head spinning.

His hands drop, and the loss of physical contact between us has my emotions heightened.

"Of course," he says, as I rush to my feet. "Allow me to walk you there."

"No," I firmly reply, heading toward the door. "I'll be fine."

Jaxon catches my arm, and brings me against his chest. "Are you leaving me?" he asks, quiet, concerned. "Or, are you coming back?"

Unsure with my answer, I fretfully blink up at him.

"Yes."

His mouth turns to a firm, straight line. I must be an open book right at this very moment, unable to mask my features even the slightest. I am utterly screwed.

"Yes, what?" he asks, stroking my hair. "Sasha?"

"Yes, I'm coming back."

And there it is.

A DULL RINGING settles in my ears as I tune out everyone in the dining area, weaving in and out through the tables like a madwoman. Nearly stumbling on my heels, finally, I reach the secluded restroom area. The lights are dim hanging against the walls, and I enter the woman's bathroom struggling to catch my breath.

"Shit," I gasp, running my fingers through my bouncy waves, trying desperately to calm myself. "Fuck. Fuck!"

The sound of a toilet flushing sounds, and an elderly woman appears from behind the door of a stall, staring at me in horror.

"Sorry," I quietly say, as she washes her hands at the sink beside me. "I am so sorry."

Completely avoiding eye contact, she exits the restroom at once.

Taking in the sight of my reflection in the mirror, I suddenly find myself questioning everything. It feels as if the wind has been knocked out of me. My palms are clammy, and my legs feel like pudding.

I'm simply terrified.

Taking in slow, deep breaths, I somehow manage to calm myself down. The truth of the matter is, I cannot let my guard down again. I cannot allow myself to feel. I cannot back down.

Gaining back control over this situation, I leave the ladies room with determination.

Hiding in the shadows of the hallway, I catch a glimpse of a figure from the corner of my eye.

Suddenly, something firmly grasps my wrist, and I'm pushed up against the wall.

There's a man standing before me, in a suit and tie, and he's tall. Good looking. The main thing that catches my attention, is the way he's looking down at me as if he's just won the lottery.

"Well," he finally speaks, while his gaze roams over what seems like every inch of my body. "You are a beauty."

"And, you are?"

He smiles, amusingly, making the hair stand up on the back of my neck.

"Who the hell are you?" I ask again, demanding.

"It doesn't matter who I am, doll."

Glaring at him, an unsettled feeling creeps up on me. "Excuse me?"

"What really matters, kitten, is how drop-dead gorgeous you are." He becomes quiet, undressing me with his eyes. "You have the most perfect legs. Beautiful, long legs."

"I'm leaving."

Turning away, he grabs me once more, pressing me into the wall with his body. He's strong, poised. A threat.

I now understand the gravity of what is happening, and my fight or flight mode kicks in.

I struggle against him. "Get your hands off me," I hiss.

"Sorry?"

"Let me go."

"Oh, you're a feisty one," he groans, smiling.

"Let me go!"

"Beg."

"Get the fuck away from her," Jaxon commands. Threatening, powerful, vicious.

The man immediately releases me, and I take in the sight of Jaxon staring savagely at the man before us.

Jaxon darts forward, grabs him by his suit jacket, and tosses him into the wall with a *slam*.

"Who the fuck do you think you are?" Jaxon growls, ominously, demanding an answer. "Don't you ever touch her again, or I'll fucking kill you."

"Jax," I gasp.

He slams him against the wall again, harder, and the loud thump makes me jump. Quickly rushing toward them, Jaxon shoots me a stare, warning me to back off.

I step back.

"Calm down, bud," the man groans, smirking mischievously. "You won't hurt me. Not here, in front of all these guests."

"Do you want to fucking test me?"

The man gives up, holding up his hands in defeat.

Jaxon releases him, shoving him across the hallway. Suddenly, his eyes lock with mine. Before I can even make sense of it, Jaxon strides over to where I'm standing, and brings me closer.

"Are you okay?" he quietly asks.

"I'm fine," I stammer.

Taking my face between his hands, he searches my eyes. "Did he hurt you?"

"No."

"Am I sensing admiration?" The man chuckles, taunting him. "You mean to tell me you actually care about this slut?"

Jaxon turns without the slightest bit of warning, and his fist meets the man's face with a crunch. Grasping his nose, blood pours from it like a faucet, and he slumps to the floor.

"I'm sorry," Jaxon says, blocking my view. "I am so sorry this bastard put his hands on you. Come with me."

Without hesitating for another moment, I place my hand in his.

"Nice seeing you again, Jaxon," he mumbles through bloody, clenched teeth. "It's been a while, but it's always a pleasure."

Without any further words, we turn around the corner. Walking fast through the dining area, my thoughts are now on overload, and my stomach is in knots. After believing they were strangers to one another, I couldn't have been more wrong.

They know each other, and I can't help but wonder what the mystery man's intentions truly were.

If only I knew.

CHAPTER 22

*T*here are reporters and cameramen gathered along the sidewalk as we step outside the restaurant. Within seconds, Jaxon is recognized, and an army of paparazzi begins to scurry in our direction.

He leans down just in time, and presses his lips beside my ear. "Look down, and walk fast."

Jaxon swiftly removes his jacket and shields my face to the best of his abilities. Soon enough, they have us swarmed. There're flashing lights and loud chatter, as I keep my focus on the concrete ground. Gripping his jacket and pulling it further over my head, he leads me safely to the limo.

"Mr. Edwards, who is this woman you are with?"

"Would you care to share with us if you're now in a relationship?"

"Why are you trying to hide the fact that you're officially dating?"

"Who is this young lady, Mr. Edwards?"

So many questions, with no answers.

Never having experienced an encounter like this before,

I'm left with an intense rush of adrenaline. My pulse accelerates, and my blood feels as if it's been set on fire.

Climbing into the limo, I scoot as far as I can from the door, more than fortunate for the heavily tinted windows. It's a bizarre scene outside, as the reporters try desperately to get a statement from Jaxon. Even bystanders are interested as they hurry toward the large group of people, sporting excited smiles, and eager eyes.

Without saying a single word, he hops inside and casually shuts the door.

Jaxon lifts his head and looks past me. "Jonathon, will you roll up the partition, please?"

He nods. "Of course, Sir."

With that, the window slides up, granting us our privacy.

There's a dull, overwhelming silence as time slowly passes by. He appears angry, and distant, sitting as far away from me as possible. Not even looking my way once, his gaze remains on his tightly, balled up fists on his lap. Tension builds and builds, to the point where I simply can't take it anymore.

"Jaxon," I quietly speak up. "It's okay."

"No," he growls. "It isn't okay. Nothing about this goddamn evening is okay."

"That was a lot of reporters. Does that happen often?"

"No. That hasn't happened in years."

I sigh. "Well, I'm sure they didn't see my face—"

"I'm not concerned about that."

"Then, what's wrong?"

"Another man put his hands on you," he sharply breathes, setting his eyes on mine. "And I wasn't there to protect you."

"But, you did protect me. You got there just in time, and you must have broken his nose from the looks of all that blood."

His eyes grow wide, dark. Empty. "He deserved much worse than that."

"Well, I beg to differ."

"He called you a slut."

"I've been called a lot worse," I press.

"I should've killed him for touching you," he says, through clenched teeth. "I'll fucking kill him."

"Will you come here?"

Jaxon lifts his gaze, and it's more than evident that my sudden request has left him baffled.

His brows furrow, and he remains still.

Cautious.

And he looks away, releasing a sharp, shallow breath.

"Please?" I quietly add in.

Sitting beside me, he studies my every movement. Reaching up, I lightly cup my hand against his face, and his eyes glow.

"Thank you," I whisper.

He appears startled, taken back. "Don't thank me." When I begin to lower my arm, he catches my wrist. "All I want is to keep you safe. Do you understand?"

I slightly nod.

"Do you understand, Sasha?"

"Yes," I murmur. "I understand."

"You are mine. Mine to touch, mine to fuck, and mine to protect, at all costs."

He releases my wrist, and leans back against the seat.

Something in me changes instantaneously. You can almost feel an electrical current in the air, with one single spark we would surely go up in flames.

There's a magnetic pull, a force so powerful I can hardly contain myself as my hand finds his knee.

My fingertips slowly inch up his thigh, hovering over the button of his dress pants. I wait for him to stop me.

Although, he doesn't.

Meeting his hypnotic blue eyes, he remains motionless,

urging me to make a move. I'm so brutally tempted, yet I'm trying desperately to fight my reckless impulses.

This is unlike me. What am I doing?

I'm drowning in his shameless stare.

He grabs the back of my neck, his lips only inches from mine. His gaze blazes through me, swallowing me whole, pulling me from the darkness.

Pressing his lips on my throat, my body trembles. I fist his hair, relishing the scent of his favorite cologne. Jaxon eases me onto my back and hovers over me, trailing a path of soft kisses to my collarbone. He yanks my dress up to my waist, and slides my thong down my legs.

His fingertips graze my inner thigh, and my eyes squeeze shut. Rubbing my clit in precise circles, my legs spread wider. Needing more. Aching for it, craving for it.

He dips his finger inside me, stroking my walls in all the right places, over and over. Writhing beneath him, his lips find my shoulder, then my collarbone.

His fingers sink into me deeper and deeper, from slow, and steady to an urgent, torturous rhythm. My fingers claw at his chest, fisting the front of his shirt as my legs begin to shake.

"You're so fucking beautiful," he breathes against my neck, curling his fingers, stroking just the right spot. "I am the only man who can touch you this way. The only man to give you pleasure."

I moan, and my stomach quivers.

"You're mine," he whispers beside my ear. "I want to feel you all over my fingers. Come for me."

Trying desperately to stifle a cry, I bite my bottom lip, giving in wholeheartedly to each sensation as my stomach tightens. Reaching my peak, my entire body convulses.

My back arches, my inner walls clench around his slippery fingers, spasming, and my mouth falls open.

"Oh, fuck," I whimper, burying my fingers through his hair. "God, yes."

Wave after wave of intense euphoria, I ride out my orgasm, crying out to him. Gasping for air to fill my deprived lungs.

Jaxon unbuttons his pants and slightly pulls them down, hovering over me once more. Spreading my legs with his knee, he rubs the tip of his cock against my sensitive clit and wet entrance, again and again.

My hips buck against him, begging for him. For all of him. He sinks into me, slowly. I accept every inch, savoring the feeling of his full possession.

He thrusts inside of me, and firmly holds my jaw, staring straight into my eyes. Watching me intently.

My heart hammers, and I don't dare to look away as his fingers lock around my throat.

"Mine," Jaxon breathes, leaning closer, our lips only inches apart. "You're fucking mine."

I whimper, grasping his wrist with both hands, urging him to hold me tighter. The pressure increases, but it's not enough. I want more. I *need* more.

Suddenly, he flips me over.

On my hands and knees, he enters me with one, hard thrust. Tightly gripping my hips, he thrusts deeper.

Gasping for air, crying out, and squirming helplessly against him, he continues to slam into me. Over and over.

He grabs a fistful of my hair, and leans his chest against my back, the weight of his body forcing me onto my stomach.

"Beautiful," he says beside my ear. "You're so fucking beautiful. Please, come with me."

Suddenly, I'm right there with him. We find our release together, crying out each other's names.

Reality sets in, as I lie silently beneath him.

This was sensual.

Intimate.

This shouldn't have happened.

"Jaxon," I abruptly say, my thoughts racing.

He immediately withdraws himself, and sits back, breaking our physical contact.

"Sasha," he murmurs, watching me closely.

Sitting up slowly, I pull down my dress, and he fixes himself in his pants. The limo is quiet, and tensions are high. Unsure as to what just happened between us, I hesitantly gaze out the windows.

My heart is heavy. So fucking heavy.

"Sasha," he calls my name again, unsure. Concerned.

My throat closes, and I'm unable to say a word. Allowing my mind to draw a blank, my wall builds back up, and I watch the cars gliding by us on the highway.

The moon is full, and it's so bright, lighting up the night sky. Words can't even explain how beautiful it is.

"Is something wrong?"

"No," I dryly mutter, numb. "Why do you ask?"

"Forget it," he dismissively says.

And we sit in silence.

THE NEXT MORNING, I find a note on the kitchen counter.

Sasha,
At work for the day. Meet me in the playroom tonight. I want you unclothed, ready for me, on your hands and knees.
Seven o'clock.
Jaxon

CHAPTER 23

*T*he time arrives.

Shutting the playroom door behind me, I raise the dim lights, and make my way to the middle of the room. My nightgown pools at my bare feet. Dropping to my knees, I press my palms into the carpet. It feels so soft.

There's an aroma of leather, and polish. The room feels dense, unoccupied. Even though I know I'm here, breathing, and living, I don't feel like I am. I'm an object, amongst the intimidating equipment hung lifelessly from the walls.

I don't know what's real, anymore.

There's such a strong silence as the minutes pass. I can hear my heartbeat, loudly thumping, reminding me to breathe.

When suddenly, the doorknob begins to turn.

Jaxon quietly enters the room.

His presence is brooding. Something thickens in his eyes, while he peers at me, taking in the sight of me completely exposed, kneeling before him. His scrutiny forces me to lower my gaze from his eyes to his solid chest, then to the bulging muscles in his arms. Black, leather pants are hung low on his hips.

Jaxon Edwards is in his element. That is a fact.

He stands before me for a moment, and then kneels. "I fucked up in a meeting today. I still managed to get what I wanted in the end, but the fact of the matter is, I fucked up, Sasha."

I'm drawn to the endless depth of his eyes, unable to speak.

"I couldn't concentrate." He trails the tip of his thumb against my parted lips. "Do you know why?"

"No," I whisper.

"Because, I was too busy thinking about you," he says, grimacing. "You and your flawless body, pinned beneath me. Your soft lips, and your beautiful, caramel eyes."

I shudder.

He stands. "On the bed," he commands, emotionless. "Now."

"Yes, Sir."

My back sinks into the mattress, and I embrace the feeling of the satin material against my skin.

Jaxon strides over to the bureau, and shuffles through a drawer. Making his way to my side, he places several objects onto a metal stand. My eyes widen with suspense.

He studies my face for a moment, and then reverts his attention back to the tray. There are long, thin candlesticks, a box of matches, and a black zipper pouch.

"Temperature play," he says, lighting a match.

"Wax play?"

"That's right."

Lighting the wick, he tips it sideways, and tests the temperature on the inside of his wrist.

His eyes meet mine. "Do you have any questions?" he asks.

"No."

"Hold out your arm."

I obey, impatiently waiting, writhing on the bed. The wax drips against my inner wrist, and there's heat, along with a burst of brief pain. The sensation is enticing, it's simply exhilarating.

It's unlike anything I've experienced.

"How's the temperature for you, Sasha?"

"Hot."

He arches an eyebrow. "Too hot?"

"No. It's fine, Sir."

Without saying a word, he places the lit candle into a holder, keeping it upright. Jaxon unzips the long, black pouch, and slowly unfolds it. My chest tightens, and a small gasp escapes my lips. My initial reaction is shock, and then *fear*.

Surely, my mind must be playing tricks on me.

It must be.

"We'll also be playing with knives," he announces, his eyes guarded, showing not even the slightest hint of emotion.

Or, not.

My heart hammers. Everything around me becomes a blur, my vision, my purpose. My life.

"Knives?"

He cocks his head to the side, and observes my reaction. This time, his eyes are cold, uninviting.

He's upset. I can feel it, radiating off him.

"That's right," he says, slowly sliding the tip of his finger against the flat surface of the blade. "Knives."

"Why?" I ask.

There's a sparkle within his icy, blue irises. He appears intrigued, entertained by the horror I'm now engulfed with. I'm drowning before him, entirely submerged.

Finally, I *feel* something.

"Oh, Sasha," he breathes, twisting the knife between his long, lean fingers. "Are you frightened?"

Yes, I mentally scream. I'm more frightened than I've been in years, but I can't admit this.

For some reason, he doesn't mind my silence.

"Don't be." He lightly places the knife back onto the tray. "Remember to use your safe word if you believe it's needed."

Squirming against the satin sheets, I am breathless.

Watching him stride across the room to a wall, he retrieves several ropes of different sizes, and I am a quivering mess. Resting the rope on the bottom of the bed, Jaxon becomes still, eying me attentively.

"Do you consent to this, Sasha?"

Without thinking it through, I nod. "Yes, Sir."

Staring at me blankly, he nods once.

Jaxon fixes the loop of the rope around my ankle, and ties it tightly to the bedpost. He does the same to my other leg, before collecting the last two ropes. Within minutes, my arms are secured as well, the rope cutting into the sensitive skin on my wrists.

"You will use green, yellow, and red," Jaxon states, with not a shred of empathy. "Green ensures it's a safe zone. When you say yellow, I will lighten up, and slow the pace. And then, there's red."

"Red means you'll stop?"

He nods. "The play will end. Immediately."

"So, I call red if I'm hurt?"

"No," he speaks over me. "That would be when you would use your safe word, Sasha. Red means you've had enough, it's become too much, and you're physically and mentally incapable of going any further. It does not imply that you are hurt."

"Red is end game."

"That's right."

Gazing deeply in his eyes, I search for something. Anything.

Although, there's nothing.

He's in his zone, incapable of emotions. And here I am, *feeling*, begging for mercy, wanting nothing more than to be untied and dismissed from his playroom. There's no escaping him. I cannot give in to the horror he's unleashed upon me.

I will not back down.

I need to do this.

The blindfold is secured around my head, cutting out the light. I'm as helpless as one could be.

"Are you ready, Sasha?"

A rush of adrenaline pumps through my system.

"Yes, Sir."

There's a hot sensation beside my belly button, and it subsides so quickly I don't even have time to react. Then, there's another, much sooner than I had anticipated. Instinctively arching my back, I tug on the ropes, stunned by the feeling. This is so unfamiliar, erotic.

With each drip of wax, all seeming to connect in a path, I'm overtaken by waves of euphoria. The purest rush of bliss. Traveling from my belly, to my ribs, the beautiful torment continues.

I am infatuated.

"Green," I purr, squirming.

"How does it feel?"

"Incredible."

"Do you want more?"

Whimpering, I take my bottom lip between my teeth. "Yes, Sir."

"Good girl."

The wax trickles along my chest, torturously making its way to my breasts. My body is trembling, and my thighs are wet. I am more aroused than I ever thought possible. Hissing, from just the right amount of discomfort, my arms stir above me.

My endorphins are released, consuming every fiber of my being, and I am enthralled. The excitement of not knowing what to expect next has me begging for much, much more.

Suddenly, something sharp presses against my skin, and trails along my ribs.

The knife.

The warmth of the candle wax returns, and my muscles relax. It's soothing, yet exhilarating, as it lightly travels in circles around my breasts. The second the wax falls onto my puckered nipple, hardening around it, I cry out to him.

There's a hot drip against my inner thigh, and every nerve is on edge, spiraling out of control. My clit is swollen, and my pussy is throbbing, pleading for more of his delicious attack.

A slice against my hip catches me completely off guard. It burns, and burns. My breathing has become labored, and my blood is pumping vigorously inside my veins.

There's another slight sting, trailing slowly down my sternum, and the pressure increases with each passing second.

I wonder if he's drawing blood.

"Yellow," I gasp.

The warmth returns between my slick thighs, teasing me, tossing me closer to the inevitable orgasm that's calling out my name.

Green, green, green.

Suddenly, there's a sharp cut against my chest, an unsettling pain. My thoughts are scattered, yet all I can seem to focus on is the fact that Jaxon could really do something like this to me.

Even if I wanted this, this is too much.

This time, he's gone too far.

"Red," I shakily say.

Jaxon removes the ropes from my sore wrists and ankles, and I tear off the blindfold in horror. Sitting upright, and staring down at my unharmed, naked, wax-covered body, I am at a loss for words.

Our eyes connect, and I am frozen in place.

Jaxon stands beside me, motionless. Quiet. Calm. Blowing

out the candle, he places it back into the holder. The knives are zipped in the pouch on the tray, and there's nothing sharp in sight.

"I don't understand," I softly say. "You cut me. I felt it."

"Did you?"

"Yes."

Slightly tilting his head to the side, his eyes narrow. "Or, perhaps, I only made you believe you were being carved."

What could he possibly mean? I felt the tip of the blade digging deeply into my flesh. Pulling his arm out from behind his back, he holds out a beautiful, red rose between us.

"For you," he breathes.

Carefully accepting the flower, I admire its beauty, and innocence.

How?

As if he's reading my mind, he speaks up. "The bottom."

That's not possible.

"You don't believe me?" he asks. "Try it."

Lightly tracing the bottom of the stem against the inside of my arm, it feels sharp, harmful. Although, it doesn't leave a mark. My mind has been playing tricks on me this whole time.

I've been mind-fucked by my Dominant.

He sits close beside me. "I would never hurt you, Sasha. You're safe with me."

Lowering my gaze to the rose, I begin to battle my inner demons. Safe with him physically? Maybe that's so. Maybe he would never cut me with knives, or whip me so savagely that I would be left with welts all over my back.

However, safe with him mentally? Emotionally?

To trust this man with my heart?

I could *never*.

Jaxon would like to go back to the way everything was before our morning at the cabin, but I wouldn't be able to bear it. This man only wants me for one reason and one reason only.

To be his submissive.

With no chance of a future, I could never let my guard down again.

I wouldn't be able to bear it.

"Tell me what you're feeling," he says.

I feel numb. Mind, body, and soul. I'm lost, in a world of chaos and fear, and I don't know how to find my way back home. Except, this isn't home. This will never be my home.

"Nothing, Sir."

He sharply exhales. "I should punish you for your dishonesty."

Lifting my head, I stare vacantly into his eyes. "I feel nothing."

"You consented to knife play. You didn't even ask questions," he says, rushing to his bare feet. "Tell me why."

My mind wanders.

"Tell me," he orders, his voice booming.

He's upset. This is clear.

"Because I trust you," I reply, but it sounds more like a question than an answer.

"You and I both know that's far from the truth."

Well, he's not wrong.

The truth is, I didn't consent to this because I trust him with a blade. I'm so broken, and empty, that I would rather feel anything than deal with the burden of feeling nothing.

Even if it's pain.

This is my one moment of weakness, an undeniable craving I could not resist, even if I had tried.

My breath catches in my throat from the heaviness in the room, from this confrontation I so desperately would like to avoid. I emotionally and physically can't do this.

I'm drained, utterly exhausted.

And he is, too.

I can see it behind his eyes. The mask he's been wearing has lifted, and here he is, desperately standing before me. Hands by his sides, balled into tight fists, brows furrowed. His jaw is clenched hard, twitching. He's peering at me, with those sharp, blue orbs, disturbed by my lack of emotion.

Fidgeting with the rose, I choose to not speak a word. There's nothing I could possibly say in this moment to make things right. Jaxon gazes meaningfully into my eyes, before turning away.

And I'm finally left alone.

CHAPTER 24

*J*axon and I have hardly spoken for the last three weeks, and other than our heated encounters in the playroom, our Dominant and Submissive relationship has been just that. A binding contract.

Nothing more, and nothing less.

Jaxon has barely kept in touch with his family, and the times that he has been in contact with them, he's come up with excuse after excuse as to why we can't make it. I haven't asked any questions, because deep down, a part of me knows why.

He doesn't want to take any chances, not with how I've been acting lately. It's been all about business between us, with silent dinners, detached stares, and an absence of interaction.

After nearly forcing myself out of bed, I make my way down the stairs, eager for a cup of coffee. Spotting Jaxon at the dining room table, I notice his cellphone pressed against his ear.

"Yes. That works," he says, lifting his gaze to briefly meet mine. "I should be leaving within the next hour or so."

Grabbing a mug from the cabinet, I turn to look at him once more, curious as to where he's going.

"Not quite sure on that yet. I'll keep you posted, Ron."

With that, he ends the call.

"Morning," I quietly speak up, initiating a conversation.

"Good morning."

Sitting across from him at the table, I focus on the steam from my coffee. Fortunately, it's still hot.

There's an intimidating silence.

"Did you sleep well?" I ask.

"No." His eyes turn to slits, and he appears distracted. "Pack an overnight bag."

"I'm coming with you?"

"You are."

"To where?"

"We're leaving in an hour," he dismissively says, before gracefully leaving the kitchen.

There's an eerie silence between us, as we drive down winding roads, and it almost seems familiar.

Once we arrive to the secluded airport, I'm struck with uneasiness. We've been here before. My thoughts become a shambled mess as I allow my gaze to roam over the vast length of his private jet.

There's a charge in the air as we sit quietly in our seats once we're aboard. I can't help but wonder where we're going, where he is planning to take me. But most of all, I can't help but wonder why he won't speak a single word.

Jaxon continues to brush me off, even after our bumpy takeoff, completely ignoring my existence. It's evident that there's something on his mind, something he's hiding, especially considering how he's wearing jeans and a shirt, rather than his usual business attire.

It only seems to make me feel more anxious as the time passes by, after realizing how far we are traveling. Hour after hour, my head is left spinning, until I simply can't take it anymore.

Reaching beside me, I lightly touch his arm.

He flinches, startled. His beautiful, blue orbs lock with mine. Finally, I can breathe again.

"This isn't for business, is it?"

"No, Sasha," he quietly replies. "It's not."

"Where are we going?" I ask.

Disregarding my question, Jaxon turns away.

And I don't back down.

"Where are we going?" I repeat, trying my best to remain calm, although my voice comes out shaky.

He stays silent.

And my heart swells in my chest.

"Don't," I rush out, barely audible.

He stands without warning, and paces back and forth across the living area in distress.

As soon as his eyes set on mine, everything falls quiet.

Too quiet.

This isn't right.

From the way he's staring down at me, my instinct is proven accurate. We were fine before we met, and now, our lives have become disrupted. Chaotic. I'm not the only one affected in this mess. Finally, I can see everything perfectly clear.

Jaxon has been affected, too. The only worlds we've ever known now seem to spin helplessly in circles.

Far beyond our control.

I quickly stand, and hurry toward him. "Don't do it."

His face drops.

"Whatever you're about to do to me, don't," I beg.

Stepping forward, he takes my face between his hands. "You don't understand," he blatantly replies, eyes widened. "You've given me no goddamn choice."

And he releases me.

We finally begin to descend. All I can focus on is how tense

Jaxon seems sitting in the seat beside me. He shuts his eyes, pinching the bridge of his nose between his fingers.

I have never seen him this way. This is a man who has always been in control, calm and collected.

Now, he appears to be the complete opposite.

Once we step outside the aircraft, I immediately recognize where I am. My stomach turns over. It's the same private airport as the one back at home.

"New York," I blurt out. "Why are we in New York?"

He's expressionless, silent.

Finally getting a grasp of reality, I understand why he has brought me here. Just like that, our arrangement must be over.

Our contract is being terminated.

The clouds darken, and a storm approaches. There's a strong flash of lightning as the sky grumbles. Focusing on the soft pitter-patter of the rain against the windshield, it's as if the Heavens above are acting on behalf of my emotions.

There's a boom of thunder, and it begins to downpour, almond size droplets splattering against the glass.

We pull over to the side of the road, and the moment I take in our surroundings, my heart sinks.

I'm reminded of chaos, loss, and grief.

Throwing open the car door, I rush toward the black gate of the cemetery. There's a wall of water, hammering down, soaking every inch of me.

My heart swells in my chest, and tears threaten my eyes.

Memories rapidly come flooding back to me.

Memories of my childhood, the accident.

My parents.

"What is this?" I demand, horrified, turning to find Jaxon standing several feet away. "Are you trying to torture me? This is where my parents are buried!"

"I know," he breathes, reaching out to me, stepping closer.

And I step back. "Don't fucking touch me," I snap.

"Sasha, please—"

"How did you find out?" I demand, boiling with rage. "Why did you bring me here? I don't want to *feel* anything! Is that what this is?"

His lips part, although he remains silent.

"You're trying to get a reaction out of me? Is that it?"

A pained expression claims his face, and his eyes burn into mine.

"I don't know," he mutters.

"Why can't you just let me be?"

"I can't."

"Why are you doing this?" I frantically ask, thunder roaring from above. "Are you doing this to hurt me?"

"No," he growls. "I'm doing this because I care about you! Don't you get it?"

Confused as ever, I shake my head, my eyes glistening with tears.

"I don't understand. I don't understand!"

"Sasha," he speaks over me, taking my face between his hands. "I'm falling in love with you."

CHAPTER 25

My heart sinks. The wall I have built up in the back of my head, keeping me from feeling anything, comes crumbling down all at once. A rush of emotions wash over me. Confusion. Happiness. Sadness. *Fear*.

I've never been so petrified in my life.

And there's an onslaught of anger. So much fucking anger.

I'm not just mad at him, I'm mad at the whole world. I'm mad at the universe for taking my parent's away from me. I'm mad at the world for leaving me without a family.

I'm mad at this man for taking me here, out of all places, for bringing me to the cemetery where my mother and father are buried. I'm mad at him for everything.

Before I can even think it through, my arm winds back and I slap him across his face. His head flings to the side, and then his eyes lock with mine. Fear courses through me.

I've hit him…

I've hit him!

Although, he doesn't speak.

He doesn't even blink.

Jaxon steps closer, and I shove him hard in the chest. He

barely budges. He just stands strong, towering over me. I feel helpless, disgusted, completely outraged. I just want to hurt him the way I've been hurt.

The way he's hurt me.

"I hate you," I tell him, blinking back tears.

Shoving him again with all my might, he stumbles back, and I shove him again.

And again…

And again.

The darkened sky flashes, and thunder viciously roars from above. He grabs my wrist, and brings me against him. Pulling away, I fling out my arms, pounding my fists on his chest.

"I fucking hate you!"

Hating him for offering me this deal.

"I wish I never met you!"

Hating him for kissing me.

"I should've left you!"

Hating him for hurting me.

"Messing with my head, turning on me at the cabin, calling me your fucking slave!"

Hating him for bringing me here.

My fists pound harder. "How fucking dare you!"

Hating him for making me *feel* again.

Feel *everything*.

Hating him for making me feel the same way about him, that he feels about me. My mind is racing, and my ears are ringing. My heart is hammering so fast I can barely breathe.

And finally, I run out of breath, and fall into his arms. Jaxon holds me tight, so tight that I'm nearly crushed by his strength.

Tears escape from the corners of my eyes, and I cling to him for dear life. It feels like he's physically holding me together, and if he were to let go at any moment, I would fall apart.

I would crumble into nothing.

The coldness of the rain seeps through my clothes, chilling my skin. The rain beats down against the trees, splattering against the pavement, and flooding the street. All I can smell is the musky air from the rainfall mixed with Jaxon's cologne.

My favorite smell in the whole world.

He gazes down at me, and the water beads down his face, coating his eyelashes and lips.

"I can't sleep. I can barely eat," he says, cupping my face with his hand, tracing beneath my eyes with his thumb. "I'm fucking up at work, left and right. I've been spending every waking second trying to think of ways to get you back."

Blinking up at him, I am lost.

Yet, I am found.

"Don't," I desperately plead, as he brushes his thumb against my quivering lips. "Please, stop—"

"No," he breathes, his face softening. "You need to hear this, dammit. I've never felt this way before. About anyone. Never."

"You're so full of shit," I whimper, and he brings me closer.

"When we met, I wanted the challenge. I craved it," he grits out, heat in his eyes. "I wanted you. I wanted to corrupt you."

He becomes quiet, vulnerable. His eyes soften.

And it takes my breath away.

"Then I *felt* something, and I've never felt anything. I've kissed you. I've slept in the same bed as you. I've broken all my rules, for *you*, Sasha."

There's a glimmer in his eyes.

"Out of all the things in this world, you're the only thing that truly terrifies me."

"You hurt me," I say, my voice cracking. Resting my hands on his chest, tears continue to stream down my face. There's no holding them back. "I trusted you, Jaxon, and you hurt me."

"I know, Sasha." He leans his forehead against mine, and pulls me closer. "Don't cry. I'm so fucking sorry."

I whimper, taking my bottom lip between my teeth.

"With you, I'm different. You're changing me. You're changing my life," he says, staring meaningfully into my eyes. "I want you on your good days, your bad days, and everything in between. I want to protect you from all the evil things in the world. I just want *you*. I want all of you."

I cry out, sobbing. Happy. Sad. So confused.

"I—I don't know what to say," I stammer.

"Don't say anything," he replies, gently tucking a strand of wet hair behind my ear. "Just let me kiss you."

My stomach quivers, and a shiver travels down my spine. "What?" I nearly whisper.

His arm circles around my back, and with the other he lightly cups my face with his hand. My body stiffens, and I'm on alert. My knees feel like they're only moments away from giving out. My heart drums wildly.

Thump-thump. Thump-thump.

I can hear it.

Thump-thump. Thump-thump.

Feel it.

"Tell me to stop," Jaxon groans, bringing me closer. "Just tell me to stop, and I will."

Lifting my head, my eyes find his.

Thump-thump. Thump-thump.

Only, this time, it's different. It's unlike any stare we've ever shared. There's vulnerability, an undying passion. A longing for more. Everything around us becomes a blur as I become lost in his eyes, only seeing *him*.

His strong, chiseled jawline, and those full, pink lips. His dark brows, and thick lashes, surrounding those beautiful, blue irises I swear I fell in love with the first night we met.

My beautiful, smug, devious bastard.

He leans down, slowly, giving me all the time in the goddamn world to react.

To tell him no. To scream at him. To push him away.

Except, I don't. I stand perfectly still, unable to move. To think. To breathe. Shutting my eyes, I give in to the unknown.

The inevitable.

Jaxon closes the space between us, and gently presses his lips against mine. This kiss is tender, sensual.

Beautiful.

As we kiss, really kiss, everything changes.

Something inside me crashes. A splitting atom, exploding with all the strength of a shattering nucleus. After all these years, I've finally found my place in the universe.

CHAPTER 26

*H*is lips brush mine, delicately, as we share this timeless, passionate moment. Breathing him in, I melt in his arms, feeling the light inside me return as a blazing inferno. The world ceases to exist, stops on its axis, and every ounce of my fear is washed away.

My head swims, and the waves of tranquility leave me feeling as if I finally belong. There's such an intense connection between us, a mutual need. He is my salvation and torment.

I am forever changed.

Our lips suddenly part, and we take in shaky, shallow breaths. Staring into each other's eyes in awe, passion ignites. Unable to fight it anymore, he pulls me into a fiery, demanding kiss, his hands working their way around my body.

Feeling every curve, inching up my back beneath my shirt, setting my skin on fire. I moan against his lips, as my arms find their way around his neck.

He brings me closer, until there's no space left between us. All I can feel is his heart beating against my chest.

Our breaths mingle, as he presses his tongue to the seam of my lips. With a moan, I open my mouth, and his tongue lightly strokes mine. His hand travels up my spine, until he's slanting my neck back further, deepening the kiss.

I have never in my life felt something this wonderful, this powerful. Our worlds have collided, and somehow, someway, the universe has brought us together.

Our kiss breaks, and I rest my forehead in the crook of his neck. Hugging me tight, he holds the back of my head. My stomach flutters, and I am an emotional, quivering mess.

For as long as I can remember, I've been a wildfire. I did what I could to get by, and I did it with ease. I didn't have a care in the world, until I met him.

Jaxon Edwards.

He brought out a different side of me, challenged me. We challenged each other. When we first kissed, I broke my only rule, for him, because I hadn't felt anything so significant for another person since my parent's deaths.

He made me feel *alive*.

Then, I finally broke down. I fell apart right in his arms, and told him my story. I confided in him, believed that I meant something to him, and he fucking tore my heart into pieces.

He reminded me of how alone I was in this cold, cruel world, and stole away every ounce of strength I had left.

The only way to save myself was to become numb. To shut down. To hide within the darkness deep in my soul.

Finally, I see the light.

I see the rain falling freely from the sky. I see the leaves rustling on the trees from the wind. I see the stormy clouds, the gravestones beyond the gates in the cemetery, and I see *him*.

Staring emotionally into my eyes, as if I'm the center of his universe. The only thing that matters.

Before I can blink, my lips crash onto his, stealing his breath away. Savoring the taste of him, I take his collar between my fists, pulling him closer.

Jaxon groans against my mouth, deep in his chest, and lifts

me into his arms. My legs lock around his hips, as I run my fingers through his silky, wet hair. Tightening his arms around me, his tongue firmly brushes mine, and I drown in bliss.

"Tell me again," I breathe against his lips.

"I'm falling in love with you."

He kisses me hard, with an urgency, putting every piece of me back together. I softly moan, shuddering against him.

"Jax—I—"

"I don't expect you to say anything," he speaks over me, and I shiver. "Fuck. You're cold. Let's get you back in the car."

Placing me back onto the pavement, he takes my hand and leads me toward the warmth.

The air in the car is electrifying. Time seems to stop as I set my gaze on the beautiful man beside me. His grip is tight on the steering wheel, and his shoulders are tense. My thoughts are erratic, and my head is spinning far beyond my control.

We arrive at a hotel on the outskirts of the city. Thunder roars as we hurry through the front doors, seeking refuge from the storm. After leaving the lobby, we take the elevator to the fourth floor, and there's a dull silence as we step inside our suite.

Standing motionless in the center of the room, I watch him place our luggage beside the dresser. He unzips his suitcase and retrieves a white t-shirt before placing it onto the bed. Striding over to where I'm silently waiting, he strips me from my wet clothes and pulls his t-shirt down over my head.

Jaxon draws down the sheets and quilt, and I crawl beneath them, snuggling into the warmth.

Sitting on the edge of the bed, he tucks me in, before lightly brushing his fingertips against my cheek.

"Are you warm enough?"

Swallowing hard, I nod. "Yes."

"Good." He sighs, stroking my hair. "Rest. I'll be right here if you need me."

He stands, reaching behind his shoulder and pulling his damp shirt over his head. The muscles in his back flex as he steps out of his pants and boxers. The sight of his bare backside leaves my heart pounding.

Turning off the light, the room darkens. The only remaining light is from the window with the curtains hung to the side. It's the perfect amount.

After stepping into a new pair of boxers, he sits silently in a chair, staring down at the table's surface. He appears so torn, distracted. Finally, I realize I haven't even considered how he must be feeling.

He is a Dominant, uninterested in anything other than the BDSM lifestyle. Although, he cares about me. He wants me. He's falling in love with me. And there's no sense in trying to hide it any longer.

I'm falling in love with him, too.

Staring at him from across the room, the complete and utter silence comes to an end. A gasp escapes from me. His head snaps up at once, and his troubled eyes burn into mine.

And he *knows*.

Jaxon's face softens, and his lips part, creating the perfect O shape. His brows furrow, and he studies the look on my face, before pushing out his chair.

Standing still, he watches me intently. I don't protest as he strides over to the bed, lying in the vacant spot beside me.

Turning his head, our eyes meet. The spark in the air returns. It feels like our souls have connected on a whole new level.

Gently brushing the hair away from my face, he stares longingly into my eyes. Leaning closer, inch by inch, my heart hammers. Until finally, he closes the space between us and presses his lips against mine.

CHAPTER 27

*W*ithin a few hours, the storm passes. Standing outside on the balcony, I take in the sight of the city out in the distance, overtaken by memories of my childhood. This time, instead of pushing them away, I choose to accept them.

Holding them close to my heart.

Feeling a presence behind me, I turn to meet Jaxon's caring eyes. Standing in the doorway, he remains silent. Making his way beside me, he places his hand on the small of my back.

His touch feels incredible. Shutting my eyes, I take in a deep breath, willing myself to be strong. He rubs my back, comforting me in a way words cannot.

"How are you feeling?" he asks.

"I'm okay," I softly reply.

"Good." He grins briefly. "I had planned on us spending the night here, but a meeting was just scheduled for tomorrow."

"I understand."

"Would you like to try again?" he questions, and I stay

quiet, struggling for words. "It's all right if you're not ready, Sasha."

"I am," I rush out, weakly grinning. "I'm ready."

THE COOL AND musty air greets me as I step out of the car. My gaze sets on the black gate of the cemetery, and my heart immediately sinks.

It's been years since I've visited where they're buried. All my bottled-up emotions are finally spilled out as tears spring to my eyes.

"Are you all right?" Jaxon asks.

"I'm okay."

With a nod, he disappears from my view. I walk forward, releasing a shaky, shallow breath. Resting my hands against the cold, metal gate, I am filled with uncertainty.

I don't know if I can do this.

The sound of the trunk closing catches me off guard. Several seconds later, Jaxon appears with a bouquet of flowers.

Red roses.

Tears escape from the corners of my eyes, and I can't help but weakly smile at his thoughtfulness.

"Jax," I whisper, and he wipes away the wetness with the tip of his thumb. "My favorite."

"I know," he replies, crookedly grinning. "Are you sure you're ready to do this?"

Swallowing hard, I nod. "Yes."

"I'm here for you. You don't ever have the face this alone again."

He leans down, planting a soft kiss against my forehead. Linking my arm through his, we quietly make our way through the gates.

Once we arrive before their headstones, everything else

becomes a blur. All I can focus on are their names printed in capital letters across the stones.

RICHARD PAUL PIERCE.

MICHELLE DIANE PIERCE.

Squeezing my eyes shut, I can see their faces. I can hear their voices. It's such a calming, reassuring moment for me.

It's finally time to allow myself to grieve.

Spinning around, I lock my arms around Jaxon's waist, burying my face into his shirt. His embrace feels so warm and I have never felt so safe.

This is right where I belong.

Right here, in Jaxon Edward's arms.

"My birthday," I stammer, staring up into his eyes. "The anniversary of their death. It's only a little over a month away."

He holds me closer, stroking my hair. "It will be okay."

"Thank you," I murmur, accepting the flowers, breathing in their beautiful scent. "For bringing me here. For caring. For the flowers." I smile down at them. "They're beautiful."

"Anything. I'd give you anything. Anything, and everything."

Gazing into his endless, blue orbs, I melt inside.

Turning back to their gravestones, he patiently waits, staying true to his word. He does not leave my side. I step closer, tears pouring from my eyes, soaking my cheeks.

Leaning down, I place the flowers onto the ground between their tombstones in a heavy daze.

They deserve gorgeous, expensive headstones, unlike the ones I had chosen for them at that traumatic point in my life.

They deserve so much better than this.

They deserve to be alive.

I whimper at the thought, pressing my hand against the cold, rough stone, breaking down. My cries are muffled, and my chest aches. I cry with everything in me, sobbing like a baby.

"Sasha," Jaxon murmurs, holding onto my shoulder.

Placing my hand over his, I cry harder. Painfully, until it's a struggle to even breathe.

He helps me to my feet, and brings me against him, hugging me tight. So, so tight.

Although, that's just what I need right now.

I need to be held, to be loved. And for once in the last seven years, I feel as though I finally belong.

STEPPING INSIDE THE JET, everything is different. The chemistry between us is higher than imaginable. It feels like there's an electrical current in the air. The hair stands up on the back of my neck, and a shiver travels down my spine.

Suddenly, our eyes lock. My knees grow weak from the intensity of his stare. Without saying a word, he takes my hand and leads me down the hall.

My stomach drops the moment we step inside a room. His room. As shocked as ever, I patiently stand beside his bed, not making a single movement.

He quietly shuts the door behind us, and my heart races. Slowly making his way toward me, he stops mere inches away. I've never been more on edge. I'm overwhelmed with feelings that I've never felt before, beautiful yet terrifying feelings.

For once in my life, instead of running from them, I decide to listen to my heart.

"Make love to me, Jaxon."

A fire lights in his eyes. Taking my face between his hands, our lips collide. He peels off my clothes and his pants between breaths, kissing me passionately, his hands roaming all over my body.

We gracefully fall onto the bed, sinking into the mattress. Pulling his shirt over his head, I moan against his lips. My hands roam along the muscles in his arms, slowly trailing up further to his broad shoulders.

Groaning into our kiss, he takes my bottom lip between his teeth. I grasp the hem of his boxers, tugging them. Desperate for him. He removes them, and we slip under the sheets. His smooth lips crash against mine, and he growls into my mouth, running his fingers through my hair.

Our bodies are bare, pressed tightly together, and his skin is scorching. Chest to chest, legs intertwined. Every breath taken as one.

"Oh, Sasha," he breathes into our kiss. "The world's a better place when I'm with you."

His erection rests between my thighs, and he thrusts his hips forward, rubbing himself against my slick folds. The friction feels incredible. To die for.

His lips find my neck, sucking, nibbling, trailing his way down to my shoulder. I moan in ecstasy, pushing my lower half against him.

Closer...

Closer.

Kissing his way eagerly across my chest, he massages my breasts, cupping them firmly. Quiet moans come from his throat as his lips circle around my nipple, flicking the tip of his tongue against the puckered bud.

Leaning my head back further into the pillow, my mouth falls open. I whimper, embracing the incredible sensations. My stomach quivers, and my mind wanders.

He slips his finger inside my core, gently stroking my walls. Slowly. Torturously. All I can focus on is the pleasure he's unleashed upon me as his warm lips trail down my sternum, my abdomen, and my hip.

Kissing his way down my body.

My back bows as his lips press against my inner thigh. Thrusting his finger deeper inside me, he adds in another. Goosebumps rise on my skin from the warmth of his breath. I shudder, squirming, and he spreads my legs further.

A hushed moan escapes me the moment his tongue presses against my swollen clit. Flicking lightly, slow, and steady. The perfect rhythm. He sinks his fingers into me, over and over, twirling his tongue over my sensitive bundle of nerves.

My stomach tightens. My breathing is labored. I've never felt anything this intense in my life. His tongue moves faster, matching his thrusts with his fingers.

An earth-shattering climax builds and builds, until suddenly, I'm right there. Running my fingers through his hair, I ride his face, entirely consumed by my orgasm.

I can't breathe. I can't think.

I just *feel*.

I feel everything.

Coming for him, harder than I ever have, I shatter into millions of pieces. Spiraling, flying. My body trembles. Legs shaking, toes curling.

And he groans against my sex, pulling me closer.

Bucking my hips, I cry out, pushing myself against his face as my inner walls clench around his fingers, holding them captive. Savoring every possible second of this everlasting euphoria.

Just when I've reached my peak, and can't take it anymore, he grabs my arms and holds me down. Pinning me to the bed until I'm left panting. Writhing against his mouth, and whimpering, I am helpless to this beautifully, torturous attack.

"Fuck," he growls, taking in the sight of my flushed face. "You're the sweetest thing I've ever tasted."

Releasing my arms, he moves up my body, and plants a soft kiss beneath my ear.

"You are so goddamn beautiful," he murmurs. "So beautiful."

"I want you," I whisper, resting my hand against his face.

His eyes close, and he lets out a small breath, turning his head to kiss my palm.

"You already have me."

His lips crash against mine, and I'm desperate to feel him. To touch him. Pressing my hands against his chest, his skin feels as if it's on fire.

Trailing my fingertips down the rippling muscles of his abdomen, and over the curve of his hips, my breathing quickens.

Unable to hold myself back, I wrap my fingers around his shaft. He's so hard, massive, and smooth beneath my palm, as I stroke him from tip to base.

He groans against my lips. "Fuck."

Sliding his hand between my legs, he positions himself, the tip of his crown teasing my slick entrance. He pushes in the barest inch. My walls tighten, sucking at his cock. Pushing forward another inch, my moan echoes through the room.

Aching for more.

Our lips part, and my desperation lights a fire in his eyes.

"Please," I gasp, squirming against him. "I want you."

"All of me?"

Much, much more.

"Yes," I croak. "Yes, Jax. I want you."

He carefully sinks into me, until he's buried to the hilt. Consuming me, stretching me wider. I moan as he pushes into me, over and over, until he swallows my cries with a fiery kiss.

Brushing his tongue against mine, he thrusts his hips forward, plunging himself deeper. Flutters rise in my belly, and my muscles spasm as I adjust to his size.

His lips trace along my jaw, beneath my earlobe, and my neck. Each movement is slow, deliberate.

Passionate.

His head falls into the curve of my neck. "Fuck, Sasha," he whispers, entering me hard, jolting my back into the bed.

I cry out to him, squeezing my eyes shut.

"No," he breathes, his hand cupping the side of my face. "Your eyes. I need to see the look in your beautiful brown eyes while I make love to you."

Staring into them, the room darkens.

All I can see is him.

He withdraws himself, and rolls us over, until he's lying on his back. My thighs straddle his waist and I position the tip of his cock at my entrance, staring innocently into his eyes.

Those piercing, blue eyes.

Lowering myself onto him, he slowly sinks into me, until I'm filled with his possession. It's such a snug fit, I can hardly bear it.

And he notices.

Wrapping his arms around my back, he brings my chest against his, slowly moving his hips to match my careful movements. Sliding up and down his length, I'm once again overtaken by waves of pleasure.

Squeezing my ass, he brings me down harder. I press my lips against his, and he kisses me back with an urgency. Relishing everything about him, my impending orgasm rushes closer.

The way he tastes. The way he smells. The way he breathes.

My heart swells in my chest.

Easing downward, he bucks his hips, locking his arms around me. Holding me close, his fingertips lightly stroke my back. Our lips part, and I sit back.

I ride him fast, bouncing on his pulsating cock, feeling him so deep I feel as if I'm about to explode. He twitches inside me, and his body shudders beneath me. My walls grip and massage him as I move my hips in circles.

Suddenly, he flips me onto my back, gaining back control. He slams into me, again and again, draping my leg over his hip to allow him deeper.

Pressing the back of my hand into the pillow beside my head, he links his fingers through mine.

I kiss his chest, his shoulder, breathing in the scent of his cologne that still lingers on his skin.

And finally, I'm *there*.

"Let go," he whispers beside my ear.

My orgasms bursts through me, violently, beautifully. Washing over my entire body like a tsunami.

Digging my nails into his back, my cries are loud until I become silent. My body becomes still. I've never in my life felt something this powerful, this meaningful. In this moment, there's complete and utter tranquility.

Nothing else matters, but *us*.

"Mine," he sharply breathes, kissing my lips. "You're mine. Only mine."

This man has unchained my mind, yet I am bound by his words.

"You." He thrusts forward, staring in my eyes as he finds his release. "It will always be you."

His body collapses onto mine, with the sheets lightly draped over our bodies. The side of his face rests against my chest, our fingers still intertwined.

Holding the back of his head with my free hand, I run my fingers through his silky, damp hair. He lets out a quiet breath, twitching inside me.

Withdrawing himself with a quiet groan, he rolls onto his back. I drape my arm over him, my hand pressed on his chest, feeling his steady heartbeat beneath my palm.

He pulls me closer, and I breathe him in, resting my forehead in the crook of his neck.

We share a comfortable silence for the next several minutes in each other's arms. My thoughts are calm, and my heart is full. I'm simply amazed, stunned with everything that's taken place.

It feels as if I'm floating on cloud nine. I am infatuated with the man lying beside me, yet weary.

Gently brushing the hair away from my face, his eyes find mine. It's almost as if he's looking straight into my soul. My breathing hitches. My heart races. For once, I no longer feel alone. Somehow, someway, we've become connected. There's not only passion built up inside of me, there's peace.

He's the missing piece of the puzzle I've been searching for. My lifeboat, in the middle of the stormy ocean. He's my compass, directing me to the shore.

And although it's the most beautiful feeling in the world, it's also the most petrifying.

"What are you thinking?" he asks, gently tracing the back of my hand with his thumb.

But I can't put it into words.

Noticing my silence, he rests his chin on my chest, and his eyes lock with mine. A small breath escapes me as I admire the depth of his eyes, and the innocence behind them.

Something I'm not quite used to.

"Should I give you space?"

"No," I rush out, smiling. "I'm just speechless."

"Are you?" he seductively asks, running his tongue over his bottom lip.

I playfully giggle. "You're ridiculous."

"Am I?"

Laughing again, I roll my eyes. "Yes."

"Sash," he nearly whispers, gazing up at me with intense eyes. "That's never…"

He becomes quiet, cautious.

I swallow hard, taking in the heat behind his stare.

Lightly kissing the back of my hand, he closes his eyes, savoring this raw moment.

"Fuck," he breathes, kissing my neck. "What did I do to deserve you?"

"Jax," I softly moan.

His lips travel across my chest. Circling his lips around my nipple, he twirls his tongue around and around. Firmly cupping my breasts, and massaging them, he kisses his way to the other side of my chest.

Flicking the tip of his tongue over the hardened bud, sucking, nibbling. Groaning heavily, growing thicker between my slick thighs.

My hands roam the muscles in his shoulders and back, and they flex beneath my touch. He plants small, teasing kisses down my sternum, slipping down further under the sheets.

My breathing quickens as he stands, lifting me from the mattress and into his arms. Placing me onto my feet once we enter the bathroom, and he turns on the showerhead.

Steam entirely fills the space around us. Pulling me into the shower, he brings me against him, the hot water trailing down our bodies. Leaning down, slowly, his heated gaze travels from my eyes to my lips.

"Fuck," he growls. "You are so beautiful."

He kisses me tenderly, cupping my face with his hands. My stomach flutters at the innocence of this moment. He slips his tongue through the seam of my lips, gaining back full control.

Wrapping my arms around his neck, his hands roam down my body. Squeezing my ass, his straining erection rests between my thighs, rubbing against my clit.

He catches my moan in his mouth, and moves me backward, pressing my back to the wall of the shower.

And I completely surrender.

CHAPTER 28

One of my hands tightly grasps Jaxon's knee, and the other grips the edge of the couch. My stomach drops from the obscene amount of turbulence we've been experiencing for the last ten minutes. Squeezing my eyes shut, I try to focus on happy thoughts to distract myself.

Watching the sunset at the beach. The scent of a coffee shop. The northern lights that I hope to see one day.

Puppies.

The aircraft sways unexpectedly, and my stomach turns over.

"Shit," I squeal, digging my nails into his jeans.

Happy thoughts, happy thoughts.

"It will pass," he reassures me, caressing my leg.

Shooting him a frazzled stare, I let out an irritated laugh. "How are you so calm?"

"I've been through much worse."

I sigh, shaking my head. "I will never get used to this."

"To what?"

"Flying," I grit out, taking in a deep breath. "I hate it. Why do you even have your own private jet?"

"Being a CEO requires frequent traveling."

"I'd take a road trip any day over this. *This* is a nightmare," I snarl, as the airplane slightly tilts sideways. "Shit!"

He lets out a laugh, and I gawk at him, baffled.

"You're laughing at me," I accuse. "This isn't funny."

"My apologies," he replies, a smirk playing at his lips.

Playfully swatting his arm, I roll my eyes. "This is not a joke. I am literally terrified for my life right now."

"You're safe with me."

"I appreciate that. But not for anything, you aren't the pilot, and you surely have no control over this storm," I press. "And it just makes it worse that it's nighttime, so we can't even see out the windows. We could be going down and we wouldn't even know it."

"I guess it's better not knowing."

My jaw drops at his dull sense of humor. "You're insane."

"If we are bound to crash, at least I can say that at the end of my life, I was a happy man."

With that, my stomach flutters. My heart dances. I can't help feeling giddy as I widely smile.

"That was so sweet," I quietly say.

He wraps his arms around me, and holds me close. "You're safe, Sasha."

Staring into his eyes, my body relaxes, and my thoughts become calm. And just like that, I believe him.

I trust him.

I trust him with everything in me.

OUR HANDS UNLOCK as Jaxon brings me over to the stool. He walks around the bar and moves behind the black, granite counter, standing directly across from me. I watch him silently as he grabs two glasses, placing them between us.

His eyes find mine. "What can I get you?"

"Hmm." I bite my bottom lip, skimming my eyes over the bottles of liquor behind him. "Anything that will get my mind off the fact that we're still flying through a storm."

"Mixed or straight?"

Arching an eyebrow, I smile. "Mixed? How about a sex on the beach?"

He nods, and before I know it, he slides the glass to me.

"I'm very impressed," I playfully say, taking a small sip, admiring the sweetness. "How'd you know?"

Smirking, he pours whiskey into his glass. "I did some bartending on the side while I was in college."

"You did?"

"I did."

"For how long?"

"About two years," he casually replies, appearing curious as he rests his arms on the counter. "What?"

"What?"

"That look."

"I'm just intrigued by you," I admit. "I still feel like I know so little about you. You don't open up often."

He finishes his drink, and begins to pour another, looking away. "I'm not used to it."

"I want to know more."

His shoulders tense, and his jaw tightens.

"Why does that bother you?" I quickly speak up.

"It doesn't."

"I saw you tense up. You don't have to lie."

Lifting his gaze, his eyes set on mine, and his face instantly softens. "It doesn't bother me," he says, resting his hand over mine. "I'm just not used to this."

"Communication? But it's in your contract."

"This is far different, Sasha," he replies, cautiously

searching my eyes. "I never talk about myself. I've never done this before. Not recently, anyhow."

"You have in the past?"

"I had a few relationships in high school and after I graduated. Although, they weren't long term."

I nod, stirring my drink with the straw. "Mine weren't either, and it was years ago for me, too."

"Do you trust me?"

Suddenly, I freeze, staring at him in disbelief.

He walks around the bar, and turns me in my stool to face him, my thighs straddling his waist.

"I need your honesty," he murmurs, cupping my face with his hand. "Do you trust me?"

"Yes. I don't know how, but yes."

He slowly leans down, hesitating, his lips mere inches from mine. "Good," he breathes. "There will be no more easing you into this. You're ready."

My heart hammers as I place my hands on his chest, staring eagerly into his eyes.

"Ready for what?"

His hand travels up my spine to the back of my neck. "It's time I show you who I truly am, without holding back."

"Why?" I ask, taking advantage of my sudden burst of confidence. "You think you'll scare me away?"

He fists my hair, and tugs firmly, locking me in place.

"I might," he says.

Fighting through the burning sensation on my scalp, I hold my breath, and remain still.

"Why didn't you show me before?" I softly ask.

"You didn't trust me wholeheartedly."

Tilting his head to the side, he studies my reaction, searching what seems to be every inch of my face. Loosening his grip on my hair, his eyes darken.

"Something's changed in you," he observes, twirling his fingers through the strands of my hair, and pulling tight.

Hard.

A hushed moan leaves my parted lips, and a state of serenity consumes me. The shooting pain at the back of my skull sends a rush of adrenaline through me, a longing for something darker.

And he knows.

Oh, he knows.

"Pain," he bites out, watching me closely. "The one thing you once couldn't bear, you now crave."

My heart fucking sinks.

He's right.

God, he's right.

He couldn't be more right.

"You need it," he breathes, pulling even tighter.

Blinking back tears from the harsh sting, I take my bottom lip between my teeth in attempt to stifle my moans. My nipples strain against my bra, and my inner thighs have become slick. I've never been so wet in my life.

So desperate.

Needy.

Suddenly, I'm an aroused, flustered mess.

"There's sadism…" He hesitates briefly, inching his other hand up my leg. "Deriving pleasure from inflicting pain on others."

My heart races.

"Then there's masochism," he says, his fingertips grazing my inner thigh. "You take pleasure in receiving pain."

"No," I try to say, until he buries his fingers deeper through my hair, applying more pressure.

I give in to the feeling, washed over by pure bliss, as my endorphins take over. Squirming in the stool, I try to convince myself that he's wrong. Although, my heavy breathing, quiet moans, and flushed skin say otherwise.

"There will be no more limiting my needs," he murmurs, caressing my thigh. "I'll show you who I really am, all while giving you what your heart desires."

Swallowing hard, I look deeply into his eyes. "You don't scare me."

He kisses my neck, trailing his warm lips along my jaw, before hesitating beside my ear.

"Not yet," he whispers.

THE HOUSE IS dark and quiet as we step inside. Exhaustion overwhelms me, and I've never been more jet lagged. After kicking off my heels, I make my way to the living room, feeling Jaxon's presence close behind me.

The moment I begin to walk up the stairs, he takes my wrist, and turns me to face him. Standing on the bottom step, I lift my head to meet his gaze, and there's such heat behind his eyes.

He reaches up to lightly stroke my cheek, and cups my face, before pressing his lips against mine.

A soft, lingering kiss, so sensual that it leaves my world spinning recklessly. My body dissolves against his, as my lips part, and his tongue brushes mine.

My heart swells in my chest, and my stomach flutters. Standing on my tiptoes, I grip his shirt and pull him closer, breathing in the scent of his heady cologne.

He wraps an arm around my lower back, and his hand slowly trails up my spine. Gripping the back of my neck, he tips my head up, deepening the kiss.

Suddenly, our lips part, and he rests his forehead against mine, holding me close.

Drawing back my head, I stare deeply into his eyes, shocked from the intensity of this moment.

"Goodnight Jax," I softly say, turning away.

He pulls me back to him, my hands pressed against his wide chest. Devouring me with his gaze, his breathing becomes labored.

"Sleep with me?" he asks.

His question steals the air away from my lungs, as I carefully search his eyes.

Noticing my hesitation, he cups the side of my face and lightly strokes my cheek.

"I know what you're thinking," he says, and the memory of the morning at the cabin replays in my mind. "That will never happen again. I promise you that tonight is different."

I blink up at him with uncertainty, locking my fingers around his wide wrist.

"I want to fall asleep with you in my arms, and I want you to still be in them when I wake up." He leans down, his lips mere inches from mine. "Sleep with me, Sasha."

As speechless as can be, I nod.

Gently taking my hand, he walks me to his room. The silence is deafening, and my heart is pounding.

Shutting the door behind us, his room is dark, except for the faintest amount of moonlight shining in through the window. Lifting me bridal style in his arms, he strides across the room and lowers me onto the bed.

Crawling under the covers, I watch as he strips off his shirt and pants, taking in the sight of his large shoulders, toned chest, and chiseled abdomen.

He climbs in beside me and brings me against him, our bodies molded together beneath the sheets. Resting my hand on his chest, his heartbeat is strong beneath my palm.

Drumming wildly.

Jaxon strokes my hair, soothing me. My eyelids grow

heavier with each passing second. He leans in and his lips capture mine, and the whole world falls away.

Drifting his hand to my hip, he pulls me closer until there's no space left between us. Our lips move in perfect sync, firmly, slowly. Warmth spreads throughout my body, and I sink into his hold, clinging to him. Holding onto him for dear life.

After stripping us bare, he moves onto me, crashing his lips against mine. He aligns himself with my entrance and thrusts inside of me with one, long stroke. Swallowing my moans, he pushes into me again, filling my aching void.

He kisses my shoulder tenderly, before resting his forehead in the crook of my neck. Gripping my thigh, he spreads my legs wider, giving me no other choice than to take him deeper.

After everything that's happened these last few weeks, it's been a while since I've felt anything. And tonight, I *feel*. I feel everything. Every kiss. Every thrust. Every emotion.

I swore that I would never let my guard down with him again, yet that's exactly what I've done.

I've invited him back in.

CHAPTER 29

*M*y eyes slowly flutter open, adjusting to the light spilling in through the windows. A happy grin claims my face as I roll onto my back. Fear consumes me. Doubt. My heart immediately sinks, and a feeling of emptiness fills my chest.

Jaxon is nowhere in sight.

Sitting upright, the sheets pool at my waist. My naked body reminds me of last night, Jaxon making love to me, and falling asleep in his arms.

Now, I am alone.

With my thoughts racing, I anxiously look around the room, feeling betrayed. Until suddenly, Jaxon strides out of the bathroom and stands casually in the doorway.

He smiles. "Good morning, beautiful," he says, and it sounds like music to my ears.

Tears of relief spring to my eyes. "Morning," I softly say, watching him closely as he makes his way to my side.

Frowning, he sits on the bed, cupping my face with his hand. "Is something wrong?" he asks, startled. "Are you okay?"

I nod, my eyes glistening in the sunlight.

"Well, which one?"

Laughing under my breath, I lift my hand to lock my fingers tightly around his wrist.

"You're okay?" he asks, grinning.

"Yes," I reply, widely smiling. "I'm okay. I just woke up and you weren't next to me."

"I'm so sorry," he rushes out, stroking my hair.

"That was terrifying."

"Oh, Sasha."

He leans forward, and presses his lips against mine. He kisses me tenderly. Slowly. Breathing me in, groaning under his breath.

"I thought I had made it clear when I said that would never happen again."

"I'm just glad you're here," I sincerely say, meaning it deeply. "I'm so happy."

"You make me happy," he softly replies, tracing his thumb over my lips. "I've fucked up. I've made mistakes."

"It's the past."

"I want nothing more than to make it up to you," he says, firmly cupping my breasts, twirling his fingers over my nipples.

Biting my bottom lip, I lean into his touch. "I know where you could start."

A small breath escapes his parted lips, as he takes in the sight of me exposed in his bed.

His eyes meet mine, and there's nothing but passion. Devotion. No hint of darkness in sight.

"You are so goddamn perfect," he murmurs. "Your eyes show me the life I feel as though I don't have."

I sigh, gently taking his face between my hands. Our lips collide, and I kiss him hard. Passionately.

Desperately.

As if my entire life depends on it.

Butterflies take over my belly, and my heart flutters. And in this moment, I can feel it. There's no second-guessing it, or beating around the bush. I know that it's happened.

I've fallen helplessly in love with this man.

And there's no turning back.

HE PRESSES my back to the wall beside the front door, dropping his briefcase to the floor. Wrapping my arms around his neck, I pull him closer, pushing my body against his. My mouth opens, our tongues fighting for control, and he wins.

Oh, he wins.

He explores my mouth, brushing his tongue against mine, and I savor the feeling of his hands grabbing me. Squeezing me. Yanking me closer to his waist, his erection straining beneath his dress pants.

Moaning into the kiss, I run my fingers through his hair, my fingertips massaging his scalp. He growls against my lips, pinning my arms against the wall.

Rubbing my waist against his crotch, he releases me, trailing his hands from my hips to my ass. He pulls me closer, the friction sending sparks throughout my body. I'm on fire against him, trembling, aching.

"Fuck," he growls low in his throat, yanking up my dress when I least expect it.

He rips off my panties with one swift motion, and spins me around. Slamming the front of me up against the wall, he wraps my hair around his wrist, pulling my head back.

Firmly gripping my jaw, he kisses my lips.

"Fuck me," I groan.

The sound of him unzipping his pants leaves me with a rush, and I push my bare bottom against his waist.

"Do not move," he orders, spreading my legs with his knee.

"Fuck me," I plead, whimpering. Moaning.

"You want me to fuck you senseless?"

"God, yes."

"Beg for it," he grits out, grabbing my ass.

Rubbing it. Massaging it. Loosening my muscles, ensuring that the blood is flowing.

Panting, I turn my head to stare into his eyes.

Smack.

"Fucking beg for it," he commands, bringing his palm down on my tender bottom again.

Smack.

Smack!

Crying out to him, my head falls back in astonishment.

"Please," I quietly let out.

"Try that again."

Smack.

"Oh! Please!" I say louder, pushing back against him.

"Not good enough."

Smack.

He slips his hand between my thighs, tracing his fingers over my tingling clit. I jolt forward from the unexpected contact, shaking feverishly, whining.

He whines back, mocking me.

It only seems to make me wetter, more aroused.

"I love feeling how wet you are. Seeing the desperation in your eyes. Hearing the sound of my hand against your ass."

Smack.

"Yes," I moan, a shiver traveling down my spine.

"Did I say you could stop?" he growls, spanking me so hard I'm now seeing stars. "Beg."

"Please! Fuck me! Please fuck me, Sir," I desperately say, my lips quivering, giving in to him entirely.

"Good girl."

He rubs the tip of his cock against my wet slit and clit, sending every nerve ending on edge. My legs begin to shake violently as I press my fingertips into the wall, resting the side of my face against the cold, hard surface.

"Do you like when I tease your wet, swollen pussy with my cock?" he asks into my ear.

"Yes," I say, whimpering, as rubs his member between my slick folds. "Yes, Sir. I love it."

"Such an eager, feral, desperate little slut."

Moaning from his choice of words, the blood boils in my veins. I've never been so turned on in my life.

"You like it when I call you that?"

"Yes, Sir. I love it."

"Whose slut are you?"

Grinding myself against his leg, I whimper. "Yours, Sir."

"That's right," he bites out, pushing in the barest inch. "You. Are. Mine."

Thrusting into me, he stretches me wide. I cry out to him, filled with his invasion, my mouth falling open. He doesn't even give me a moment to adjust to his size before slamming back into me, over and over.

I grunt with each thrust, overtaken by a state of pure euphoria. I can hardly breathe, hardly think. All I can focus on is the earth-shattering sensations he's applying to my body as he fucks me harder than he ever has before. His hips slam against my ass, bruising my skin.

There're the loud sounds of praise, skin smacking, and our even breaths echoing throughout the entryway. Tightly gripping my waist, he plows into my core, my inner walls sucking at his cock. Gripping his length, massaging him. He buries himself deeper, increasing his pace, fucking me mercilessly.

Suddenly, I'm seeing stars behind my eyelids. Something inside of me explodes, shattering into millions of pieces. My moans become cries, and my body convulses, aftershocks of my orgasm rocking through me as he slams into me harder.

"Fuck," he growls, gripping my hair with one hand and my shoulder with the other, locking me in place. "Mine…Fuck."

He finds his release, shooting his cum inside of me in long spurts. Leaning the front of his body against my back, he nuzzles his face in the crook of my neck.

"I want to stay right here, buried inside of you, forever," he breathes.

"Don't go," I quietly say, feeling him twitch inside of me.

He slowly withdraws himself, letting out a sharp breath. Spinning me around to face him, he leans into me, silencing me with a kiss.

I drown in contentment, his semen trickling down my inner thighs. Resting my back against the wall, I twirl his tie around my fingers, bringing him closer.

Holding my face with his hands, he kisses me softly. Slowly.

"Don't leave," I whisper against his lips, his hands trailing down to my lower back.

He draws back his head, and stares intently into my eyes. "I won't be gone for too long," he murmurs, smirking.

"You can't reschedule your meeting?" I ask, flirtatiously smiling up at him. "For me?"

"I would do anything for you."

The promise in his voice leaves my heart racing, and the room spinning. The feeling he gives me is indescribable. He brings me to life, and ignites a burning passion in my soul. His oceanic eyes lock me in place, and I'm falling for him.

Like the falling of the stars.

For the last seven years, I've been isolated, living in a dark windowless room. And then Jaxon walks in, bringing the light and escape I've been endlessly searching for.

Saving me.

He fixes himself in his pants while I pull down my dress, my slick thighs reminding me of where he just was. My core aches at the thought, the skin on my ass still warm to the touch.

"I should return around six," he says, tucking a loose strand of hair behind my ear.

"Okay," I pout, smoothing out the jacket of his suit, and fixing his collar. "Crystal invited me out to lunch."

"Did she?"

I nod, adjusting his tie to perfection. "She wants to show me around downtown, too."

"Sisterly bonding," he smugly says, reaching into his pants pocket. "Here. Take my card."

"I'm okay," I rush out, and he frowns. "My signing bonus will take care of lunch and shopping."

"Save the bonus."

"No."

Stepping forward, he cocks his head to the side. "Did you just say no to me?" he asks, eyes narrowed.

My eyes widen with anticipation.

"Are you going to make me repeat myself?"

"No," I immediately say. "I'm sorry, Sir."

"Don't disrespect me by being prideful," he says, firmly holding my jaw. "Take my card like a good little girl, and allow me to spoil you."

"Yes, Sir," I submissively say, taking the credit card from his tight grasp.

"And what do you say?"

"Thank you."

"So polite," he says, with a twitch of a smile. "When I get home, I want you kneeling in the playroom, ready for me. Am I clear?"

"Yes, Sir. You're clear."

He smirks, before pressing a soft, lingering kiss on my lips.

WITH THE CHORUS of the birds above, the breeze feels

wonderful as it brushes against my skin. The sun is shining brightly, and there's not one cloud in the sky.

The waiter returns with our drinks, placing them onto the table before scurrying away. Crystal and I laugh at the awkwardness.

"Cheers," she chirps, holding up her drink. "To drinking before five."

"Cheers to that!"

Clink.

She smiles, her light blue eyes glimmering in the sunlight. "I'm really glad you joined me."

"Me, too. I would have been bored silly all day."

"I hate that," she mumbles, plopping an olive into her Bloody Mary. "I've been drowning in school. I feel like I study more than I ever spend time with friends or family."

"Nursing school, right?"

She nods, rolling her eyes. "Yes."

"That's a really great field to get into."

"What do you do for work?" she asks.

Suddenly, I freeze, struggling for words. "Well, right now I'm taking some time off."

"You and Jaxon are staying here in California until after the wedding, right?"

"Right," I reply with a grin.

"So, what did you do for work before your break?"

"I'm a dancer."

It slips. My shoulders stiffen, and I pray it's not visible. My stomach turns over, and my heart begins to race.

"A dance teacher," I quickly add in. "And a writer."

"That's cool. What do you write?"

"Poetry."

"Really?" she gasps, eyes widened in excitement. "Me, too!"

Shit.

I mentally scold myself for lying, considering I am the worst possible writer on the planet. Especially when it comes to poetry.

"No way," I gasp, playing along. "That's awesome."

"I used to read my poetry at this little café when I was younger. I've been wanting to do something like that again for so long. I think I'm going to write something for the wedding."

"That would be so sweet."

She grins. "Do you and Jaxon have a date set yet?"

"Not yet. We're still trying to figure that out."

"He told me a few months ago that you guys lived close to one of your favorite venues?" she questions.

I nod, sipping my drink. "Yes, it's definitely one of our favorites, but we're not sold on it. New York is beautiful, don't get me wrong, but that's just not what we have our heart set on," I anxiously babble.

Pressing her lips into a straight line, she tilts her head to the side, taking in my words.

I nervously swallow, feeling as if I'm suddenly on trial. From the way she's looking at me, something in the pit of my stomach warns me that this doesn't feel right.

She briefly grins. "But Jaxon wasn't living in New York a few months ago," she presses, stirring her drink with the straw.

My chest tightens, and all the color drains from my face. "What?" I ask, barely any sound to my voice.

"Chicago," she casually says. "He was living in Chicago."

"Yeah," I blurt out. "I know."

"You said New York."

"Wait," I say, faking confusion. "Oh! The one in Chicago? I was thinking about a different one. He took me on business with him, and that's when we found the other venue. It was beautiful. You should've seen it." I nervously smile. "Too close to the city for our liking, though."

"Of course." Her lips curl into a smile. "Debby is looking forward to meeting you."

Finally, I'm able to relax.

"I'm excited to meet her, too," I say, smiling in return. "Is she having a good time on the cruise?"

"She actually just got back yesterday."

"Did she?"

"She did. I asked her to meet us for lunch, but she couldn't make it." Crystal lowers her gaze to the table, looking over the menu. "I recommend the bacon cheeseburgers. They're seriously to die for."

"Well then, it looks like I'm getting a burger."

Lifting her head, she eyes me curiously. "Really?" she asks, laughing under her breath. "You're not a vegan anymore?"

My stomach tightens, and my jaw drops on its own accord. Suddenly, my head is spinning.

"I could've sworn that Jaxon told me you were a vegan."

I quickly nod. "I am," I reply, forcing a calm stare. "They don't have veggie burgers here?"

Dropping her attention to the menu, she flips the page, pointing under a section at the bottom.

"They do," she happily says, laughing as her eyes set on mine. "You're in luck."

"Great."

"He called me earlier today," she quietly says, her voice trailing off. "Jaxon."

Looking in her eyes, I carefully nod. "What did he say?"

"Just wanted to figure out when the next family dinner was," she replies, shrugging. "Mom is planning on having us all get together in a couple days."

I smile. "I can't wait."

Shutting the front door behind me, I rest my back against the frame, excited to be home. It's been such an incredible day and I've never been happier. Memories of Jaxon and I from earlier today replay in my mind.

My head feels light, and butterflies creep their way into my belly. His touch, his dominance, everything about him drives me insane. I shut my eyes, embracing the feeling of calm that washes over me, until there's an unexpected knock on the door.

My heart leaps in my throat, and I am overjoyed at the thought of Jaxon returning home earlier than expected. Pulling open the front door with an eager smile, my stomach drops at the sight of a young woman.

"Hello," she enthusiastically says, smiling wide. "You must be Sasha."

I've never been caught so off guard. Staring at her blankly, I grip the edge of the door tighter.

"Yes," I carefully reply. "And you are?"

"Oh, right."

She laughs, flipping her long, brown hair behind her shoulder with her polished red nails. A devious smile claims her face, while her eyes stare straight into mine.

"First, it's such a pleasure to meet you," she says. "I'm Marnie."

CHAPTER 30

I've never felt so betrayed. My lungs are throbbing, begging me to breathe, to let in a single breath of air. Although, it's impossible for me to do so. Impossible.

I love you...Marnie.

The sound of his voice is perfectly clear, bouncing back and forth inside my head. Grasping the edge of the door harder, my fingers feel like they're about to snap.

He said she wasn't real, that he had never met someone named Marnie. Yet here she is, standing only feet away. The woman he had called out to in one of his dreams.

She's simply beautiful, and the resemblance between us is uncanny. This is so twisted. This cannot be happening. Shaking my head, I stare at her dumbfounded. What strikes me as odd is the amusement plastered across every inch of her face.

"Are you all right?" Her voice pulls me back to reality, yet I feel as though I'm trapped in a dream.

A nightmare.

"Sasha?"

"How do you know my name?" I ask, demanding.

She arches her perfectly shaped eyebrow, looking at me in disbelief. It's evident that my unfriendly tone has taken her by surprise.

"Well, I believe the real question here is something entirely different," she says, her smile turning into a grimace. "Don't you agree?"

"I asked you a simple question," I retort. "How do you know my name?"

"How do you know Jax?"

My chest tightens from the way she addressed him as Jax. Not Jaxon, or Mr. Edwards. Jax.

What could this possibly mean? Does she know him on a personal level? Business level? When is the last time they've seen each other? When did they last speak? Why does she even have a nickname for him to begin with?

"Jax?"

"Well, that's his name, isn't it?" she bluntly asks.

"No," I firmly respond, standing my ground. Her face drops, and her jaw clenches tight. "It's Jaxon. Jaxon Edwards. You're here, at his residence, and I live here with him. So, I'll ask you again." I hesitate, not looking away from her eyes for even a second. "How do you know my name?"

She dramatically sighs, rolling her eyes at me. "Oh, please. Let's drop this little act, shall we?" she asks, sarcasm thick in her tone. "You know who I am, and I know who you are."

"What do you want?"

"We both know that Jaxon is a successful and handsome man. Any woman would be a complete fool to not want him," she says, hesitating, appearing aggravated. "Are you going to invite me inside or what?"

I laugh, humorlessly.

Her eyes narrow. "What's funny?"

"I would never invite you inside his house, especially when

he's not here. He won't be home until later, and I highly doubt he would want you to be in his home or anywhere near it, for that matter."

"And how would you know how he feels?" she snaps. "He's inhumane. A true sadist. He's done things, unimaginable things. He'll do them to you, too, if he already hasn't—"

"You need to leave," I urge, beginning to close the door.

"Don't you want to know who I am?"

Becoming motionless, I silently stare at her.

"I was a very big part of his life," she says, lifting her chin. "You can't deny the fact that you're dying to know more about me. You must be interested to know what I was to him."

"Well, I'm not."

Without giving her another glance, I turn away, closing the door in her face.

Pressing my palms against the door, I remain quiet. Still. Not daring to move a single inch, or make a single sound. With my mind drifting, my head becomes foggy.

She's real. This whole time, she was real.

"If you don't care to know about me now, then so be it. Here."

There's an eerie silence, and about a minute later, a small piece of white paper slides under the door. My eyes lock on the scribbled blue ink, yet I make no attempt to retrieve it from the hardwood floor.

"My number. In case you change your mind," she calls out from the other side. "And just for the record, Sasha…He won't ever be yours."

Then there's the faint sound of her heels clicking against the pavement, and a car's engine roaring to life.

Jaxon Edwards confessed his love for me. He let his guard down and told me how he felt. We have fallen so deeply for each other, and I care so much for him.

I want to give him a chance to explain himself. I want him to be the one to tell me, not her. I just want him to be honest.

After making my way to my room, I place the small piece of paper inside the drawer of my nightstand, spotting the black velvet box.

Just as I reach for it, the screen of my cell phone lights up.

One new text message from Jaxon.

I can't stop thinking about how you feel around my cock. My slut better be waiting for me when I get home like I told her to.

My body betrays me, as my skin becomes flushed. With my heart beating wildly, I text him back.

Yes, Sir.

Sitting down on the bed, I wait patiently, even though he's at work and I know it could take him forever to reply.

Suddenly, the quiet *ding* takes me by surprise.

Missing you endlessly.

My breathing is quiet, shallow. I slowly stride to the center of the room, relishing the scent of polish and leather in the air that I've become infatuated with. Opening my robe, I slide it off my shoulders as it pools at my feet. Kneeling on the carpet, I patiently wait.

Time passes slowly. My mind wanders. I have so many thoughts, so many unanswered questions. With my head spinning, I hardly notice Jaxon's appearance.

His presence is brooding, and my heart hammers as I take in the sight of his black, leather pants.

"Obeying," he says, his voice low, tight. "That's my good girl."

He stands inches away, reaching down to stroke my hair. Goosebumps rise on my skin, yet my skin feels hot. My body reacts to him in ways I never thought possible. Wetness pools between my thighs, and my mouth waters.

Stepping behind me, he ties my hair back with an elastic. He firmly grips my shoulders, massaging them, before rubbing the back of my neck. It eases my tense muscles, and feels incredible.

Suddenly, his strong hands are cupping my breasts, pinching my nipples until they pucker into hard, red buds. He rolls them between his fingers, and my breathing quickens.

"This is mine," he breathes, cupping my sex with his hand. "Am I clear?"

"Yes, Sir."

"Good girl."

He teases my clit with the tip of his finger, rotating in precise, torturous circles. Slowly pushing his finger inside of me, my walls clench around him. He thrusts repeatedly, rubbing my clit at the same time, while I squirm against him. Bucking my hips as I ride his hand, needing more.

Until at the worst possible timing, I remember how he's lied to me. Betrayed me. Withdrawing his finger, he stands.

My senses are now on high alert. Everything feels different as my heart beats more fiercely. Pounding, banging. On the verge of bursting right through my chest. Sounds become louder. I can hear him breathing, slowly taking in the air. Colors become brighter. His eyes... Oh, his eyes.

So beautiful.

So mysterious.

I'm more awake than I've ever been in my life. Adrenaline courses through me, flooding my system in seconds, urging me to make a move. To speak. Although I remain still, silent.

Vigilant.

I can feel the saliva thickening in my mouth, and my stomach turns over. My chest feels hollow. Digging my nails into my thighs, I'm almost positive I'm drawing blood. Yet, I don't bother to look.

My eyes are wide, set right on Jaxon, the man I've fallen helplessly in love with. The man I've trusted. The man who has lied to me.

Just as I begin to feel the sweat that I'm covered in, he leans down to my level and studies my face. His eyes lock with mine, drawing me in, pulling me into a trance before I look away.

"No," he firmly says, taking my jaw, demanding complete eye contact. "Look at me."

Squeezing my eyes shut, I breathe in through my nose, willing myself to obey. To pull myself together, to let this go.

But no matter how hard I try, I can't.

My eyes flutter open, slowly. "Yes, Sir."

Placing his finger under my chin, he lifts my head. "Correct your posture."

Sitting up straighter, a dull ringing settles in my ears. His face hardens, and he watches me closely. It almost appears as if he's conflicted, considering something.

He stands tall, towering over me as I remain kneeling.

"You were bound to be mine," he softly says, tracing his thumb over my bottom lip. "I will never let you go."

Jaxon moves behind me, until he's out of sight. My heart is hammering, and my pulse is loud in my ears. My breathing has become shallow and uneven.

He brushes my hair behind my shoulder. My thoughts are on overload, and my senses are heightened.

"Stand," he commands.

I do as I'm told, and he leans the front of his body against my back. My chest rises with each breath, and my body stiffens. Sensing my distress, he wraps his arms around me.

"Breathe," he whispers into my ear, his hands caressing my hips. "I want nothing more than to take care of you. Mind, body, and soul."

I tremble against him, squeezing my hands into fists by my sides. "Yes, Sir," I murmur.

"Are you okay?"

"Yes."

"Are you sure?"

"Yes, Sir," I weakly reply. "I'm okay."

"Tell me, Sasha," he deeply breathes. "If I lead you into the darkness, would you follow?"

My heart swells, feeling heavy.

Suddenly, I'm battling my inner demons. I'm fighting against my only weakness. And my weakness is *him*.

"Yes, Sir. I'd follow you blindly."

"Fuck," he growls, yanking on my ponytail, pulling my head back. "You're so beautiful."

I moan from the harsh sting at the back of my head, pain shooting through my skull.

"Do you want me?"

"Yes," I gasp, as he releases his hold on my hair. "I want you."

Suddenly, he lightly slaps me across the face.

"Do you still want me?" he asks, sounding broken. Destroyed.

My body is thick with sweat. A rush pumps through my veins like nitrous. My nipples pucker, and my body quivers. There's something so twisted about this moment, yet so beautiful. Raw.

He's trying to see how far I will go. Testing me.

"Yes, Sir," I strongly answer.

He slaps me again. "How about now?"

"Yes, Sir."

And again…

And again.

Left, left, right, left, right. Shutting my eyes tight, several tears squeeze through, while my face feels as if it's on fire. He stops, cupping my cheeks with his hands, caressing the sting away with his thumbs.

"Do you still want me?" he asks once more, his eyes burning into mine.

"Yes."

"Yes, what?"

"Yes, Sir."

He leads me to the red, X-shaped platform against the wall, and I get into position. Lifting my arm, he locks the cuff around my left wrist, and then the right. He kicks open my legs, spreading them wider, and cuffs my ankles as well.

He walks away. The sound of music catches me off guard. It's soft, hypnotic. My eyes drift shut while Jaxon massages my back, my shoulders, and what seems like every inch of my backside.

I lean back, letting out a deep sigh, feeling nothing but comfort. His hands work on my muscles tenderly, until the blood is flowing. He's so gentle, calm, in full control.

Finally, he steps back, and I grow desperate for more.

"We will start with flogging," Jaxon announces.

My heart leaps in my chest. Yes, yes, yes. With flogging, there's so much pleasure, and I've grown to adore the pain.

The first snap of the whip makes me flinch, as he lightly strikes my shoulder blades. Slow, teasingly. Trailing deliberately down my back, coming down harder with each stroke. Pulling on my wrists, the cuffs dig deeper into my skin, and my arms feel light.

Although, my head feels heavy.

My heart feels heavy.

"More," I rush out, trying to distract myself. "Please."

The flogger comes down harder, brushing roughly against my tender bottom, one strike after the other.

"Green," I hiss, squeezing my eyes shut. "Please. More."

"Green?"

"Yes."

Whish. Jerking forward, a whimper escapes my lips. My skin is burning, and it seems to last forever. *Whish.* The pain worsens, to the point where I feel like I'm being carved. I say nothing. *Whish.* I cry out, putting nearly all my weight on my wrists, my legs shaking. Almost giving out.

Almost.

"Green," I force out, breathing hard.

"Sasha—"

"Green!"

"Are you sure?" he asks, doubting me. Cupping his palm against my ass, I flinch, hissing at the contact. "Sasha?"

"Yes," I breathe, my ears ringing. "Yes, Sir. Green."

Trusting my words, he continues, using the same amount of strength that I had asked him for. Begged him for. The snap of the flogger becomes repetitive, and the feeling of my skin tearing eventually becomes numb.

"You have the most incredible ass. So red," he groans, striking me harder. "Pain." *Wish.* "You want it. You crave it." *Wish.* "It's how you cope. It's your defense mechanism." *Wish.* "You need to receive it, and I need to give it. We belong together, Sasha."

Tears leak down my face, soaking my cheeks. My heart is pounding. My arms are tingling, and my legs feel like they're moments away from buckling.

Finally, I can't take it anymore. I believed that distracting myself with agony would make this all better, that it would put everything behind me. That it would clear my memories, and we could move forward, without looking back.

But I was wrong.

At this point, I can hardly think straight. Adrenaline overtakes me, consuming every fiber of my being. Determination floods through me. I will not be weak. I will not back down. I need answers, and I need them, now.

And suddenly, I do the unthinkable.
The only thing I know that will stop this.
End this.
"Black."

~ TO BE CONTINUED IN BOOK 2 ~

ACKNOWLEDGMENTS

To my soulmate, Billy, with those beautiful blue eyes surrounded by thick lashes. Thank you for everything. For giving me ideas, pushing me to write, and for supporting me during my quarter life crisis when I quit my job to finish editing. What can I say? I was working with bread and cheese, then you gave me sauce and now I have pizza.

Mom, thank you for always believing in me, and for encouraging me to reach for the stars. I love you to the moon and back, always.

Kayla Lutz, I don't know what I would have done without you. Seriously! You have been an angel sent from above. You have helped me so much, more than words could ever explain. Thank you for all your hard work, support, and for encouraging me until the very end.

Lana Sky, besides being one of my favorite authors, you have been such a huge help in my publishing journey! Thank you for answering all my questions, giving me advice, and for supporting me every step of the way.

Charity Chimni, I am in awe. You are an absolute life saver! Your quickness, eye for detail, and positive attitude has been a breath of fresh air to work with. I am so grateful to have been told about your services! Thank you so much for your hard work and for making my manuscript the best that it can be!

To my beta readers, what more can I say than I couldn't have done this without you. Thank you for all your support, hard work, patience, and incredible feedback on my book baby. I appreciate it from the bottom of my heart. You guys are the real MVP's!

To my ARC team, you guys rock! The outpouring of reviews I've received has been incredible. I am literally at a loss for words. I'm so happy you all have fallen in love with Sasha and Jaxon's story the way I have. I can't wait to give you book two!

To my readers, thank you for reading my books. Ever since I was a little girl, I loved writing, and my dream has always been to one day become an author.

And to think it all started six years ago on Wattpad.

ABOUT THE AUTHOR

Molly Doyle's passion for writing began in her fifth grade English class. After turning to an online writing platform in 2013, Molly's works have gained the attention of more than 43 million readers. When she's not binge watching Supernatural, acting in Haunt Attractions, or drinking wine near the fireplace, she's writing Erotic Romance novels and dreaming of one day becoming a Director and Screenwriter.

More than 27 million reads online.
First time in print.

Molly loves to hear from her readers! You can reach her on social media or at realmollydoyle@yahoo.com.

facebook.com/authormollydoyle

instagram.com/realmollydoyle

CPSIA information can be obtained
at www.ICGtesting.com
Printed in the USA
LVHW041511180122
708821LV00006B/212